When Rosamund had first heard the term 'Fen Tiger', she had believed it was some form of animal—until it was explained to her that it was the name given to a type of fen man, now almost extinct, but not quite. Here and there the descendants of men who had lived deep in the trackless fenland, and who fought with cunning, craftiness, and even murder, against the land being drained, were still to be found. They were independent, often surly, and at times could call up the fierceness of their forebears . . . The fenlands had once been so wild that the inhabitants had only made their appearances in the towns on festive occasions, when trouble nearly always ensued.

Today the phrase conjured up a picture of a rough, crude individual hardly able to control the elemental urges that had at one time been allowed full sway. Rosamund felt that if Michael Bradshaw was an example of a Fen Tiger there couldn't be a wide enough distance between them. Yet her fragile, delicate-looking sister was set on hunting the tiger . . .

The Fen Tiger

Catherine Marchant

CORGI BOOKS
A DIVISION OF TRANSWORLD PUBLISHERS LTD

THE FEN TIGER
A CORGI BOOK 0 552 10074 9

Originally published in Great Britain by
Macdonald and Jane's.

PRINTING HISTORY
Macdonald and Jane's edition published 1963
Corgi edition published 1976

Corgi Books are published by
Transworld Publishers Ltd.,
Century House, 61-63 Uxbridge Road,
Ealing, London, W.5.
Made and printed in the United States of America
by Arcata Graphics,
Buffalo, New York

The Fen Tiger

1

Rosamund Morley was dreaming; she was dreaming that she was putting her signature to the bottom of a document and this document concerned Heron Mill. She was not buying the mill—it was being made over to her as a deed of gift, and the donor on this particular occasion was her uncle. Sometimes, when she dreamed this dream, it was her cousin Clifford who would be the donor, and not only would she be getting the house but him too, not as a deed of gift but as a husband, and she looked forward to this part of the dream.

This dream was as familiar to Rosamund as was the room in which she slept. It usually occurred during the early part of her sleep, and had she wakened one morning and told herself she'd never had her dream she would have been surprised and perhaps a little apprehensive—she always had her dream.

Tonight the pattern of the dream was as usual—at least up to a point. She signed the document, she kissed her uncle (it was her uncle who was bestowing the gift tonight), then, turning from him, she ran out of the sitting-room, through the low hall and to the top step leading down from the front door. There, below her, lay the garden that separated the house from the river bank. The river was narrow at this point, being merely a cut meandering off Brandon Creek, but it still needed a ferry to cross it. She could not see the little red boat below the bank, but the sunlight glinting on the chain picked out its moorings on both sides of the river. The dream was still keeping to pattern: one minute she was standing on the steps of the house, the next she was climbing the wheelhouse inside the old draining mill itself. When she reached the top she ran out on to the rickety balcony, and, standing within an arm's length of the decaying wooden slats of one of the sails, she threw her head back and laughed with pure joy. From this point she could see the world—her world. Except for the little wood across the river on the Thornby land the earth was flat as far as the eye could see. There were great tracts of yellow, and red, and brown, and patches of black, such black that no artist could have captured the depth, and intersecting the colours ran silver ribbons—the rivers. Far to the left of her the silver ribbon was broken by the high banks of weeds, that was Brandon Creek. To the right of her, away, away right, the silver was very faint, for the banks of the River Wissey were high, even wooded in parts. Then right opposite to her was the Great Ouse. Two hours run down the Brandon, but only six miles as the eye went over the top of Thornby House, the main river ran towards the sea, delayed only by Denver Sluice itself.

At this point in her dream she would drag her eyes from the landscape and call out. Whether she saw him or not she would call out, "Hello, Andrew," and on her shout Andrew would appear. He would be sitting on his tractor in the middle of one of his fields and would shout back, "Hello there, Rosie."

Although the nearest Andrew Gordon's land approached the mill was a mile away where it met the boundary of the Thornby land, Andrew and the tractor would appear in the dream to be just down below her. She would lean now through the decaying struts in the old mill wheel and laugh down on Andrew, but at this point he would not be alone, for her sister Jennifer would be sitting perched up high beside him. She would wave to them both before turning and running down the rickety stairs again, filled with such happiness that the feeling was almost unbearable, even in a dream. Jennifer had Andrew, and she had Heron Mill.

When she reached the foot of the winding stairs she knew she would be greeted by her father and that she would wave the deed of gift gaily above his head. True to pattern, she was greeted by her father, but the dream from this point changed. Instead of having the document in her hand, she saw it was in her father's hand and he had set a match to the corner of it, and as the thick dry paper crackled, the smoke obliterated him from her sight and she heard herself screaming, "Don't! Oh, Father, don't! Don't! You don't know what you're doing." And then her hands were on him and she was struggling with him to retrieve the remnants of the paper.

"Rosie! Rosie! Wake up, do you hear?"

She was sitting up in bed, being gripped by Jennifer's hands while she herself had hold of her sister's shoulders.

"What . . . what's the matter?"

"Wake up! Get up! Oh, Rosie, wake up! The house will be in flames in a minute."

Rosamund was on her feet. "Where . . . where is it?"

"Father—his bed's smouldering. I tried to wake him—I nearly choked—I couldn't get him off."

Rosamund, ahead of Jennifer and on the landing now, was met by a wave of smoke coming along the passage from the open door at the end.

Just as a few minutes earlier in her dream she had groped towards him, now, in reality, she was doing the same.

"Father! Father! Wake up. Wake . . ." She coughed and spluttered as she swallowed deeply of the smoke. Then, motioning to Jennifer, she gasped, "Pull him off."

Together they pulled the heavy inert form on to the floor, then, backing towards the door, they dragged him on to the landing.

Kneeling by his side and holding the tousled gray head between her hands, Rosamund pleaded as she looked down into the white face, "Oh, wake up! Father! Father! Wake up!" She looked quickly at her sister. "He's breath-

9

ing all right. . . . Look!" She cast her eye along the passage. "Shut that door a minute. No, wait!" She laid her father's head gently on the floor. "We'll have to throw it out—the mattress."

As they heaved the smouldering mattress from the bed and struggled with it towards the window, Rosamund could not help being amazed at the fact that the whole thing wasn't in flames, for it was burning to the touch. The window was narrow, and, although the mattress was only a single one, they had a job to get it through, and an exclamation of horror was dragged from them both as, with the first draught of air, it burst into flames.

"Oh God! It might have . . ." Rosamund closed her eyes for a moment before turning swiftly towards the landing again.

Henry Morley was still lying in the same position and the two girls stood looking down at him helplessly.

"He could die like this," Jennifer said.

"Oh, be quiet!" Rosamund's voice was curt.

"Well, what are we going to do? We can't lift him."

"We'll have to try. You take his legs."

As Rosamund put her arms under her father's shoulders and attempted to heave him upwards, and Jennifer raised his legs slightly from the ground, it was evident to them both that they could do nothing but drag him.

"It's no good."

No, it was no good. As Rosamund lowered her father to the floor again she said, "Well, something's got to be done. I'd better go for Andrew. I'll phone for the doctor from there. Andrew will come back with me. That's if he has returned from the show. Oh, I hope he has."

"Blast this leg!"

This remark seemed irrelevant to the situation, but Jennifer always used it, in times of crisis, and Rosamund said sharply now, "Stop that!" She was speaking as if she were the elder of the two, whereas she was two years younger than her sister. But it was she who had for many

10

years taken the lead in the small family. She knew too at this moment that if Jennifer had not been handicapped with her limp, an almost imperceptible limp it must be admitted, she would have had no taste for running across the fens at night, even with the moon full. And so she said quickly now, "Get some blankets out of the cupboard; it's warm, but you never know. I'll take the Tilley." She turned to where a Tilley lantern was glowing on a little table near the wall. They had made a practice of always keeping the lantern alight for just such an emergency as had occurred. At times Rosamund had been very tempted to save on the oil, but she was glad now that economy had not driven her to this false move.

She ran into her room, and, not stopping to take off her pyjamas, she dragged over them a pair of slacks and pulled on her shoes. Then, rushing on to the landing again, she was about to pick up the lantern, when she realized that in taking it she would leave Jennifer in the dark. And to be left alone in the dark would be as frightening to Jennifer as running across the fens. There was no time to stop and light another lamp, so she said quickly, "I won't bother with the lantern, it's practically broad daylight."

Jennifer's relief came over in her voice as she said, "I'll have the lamps lit by the time you get back. Hurry, Rosie; please hurry."

Rosamund said no more but ran down the stairs and into the dark hall. Groping knowingly past the table on which there were a number of brass ornaments, she opened a cupboard door and pulled out a short coat, and she was thrusting one arm into it as she unlatched the front door.

The bright moonlight illuminating the much-loved scene from the front steps did not touch her at this moment, for suddenly she was overcome with irritation and was thinking along the lines that Jennifer so often voiced. What was rural beauty if you couldn't have a telephone

11

or electric light, or electric appliances of any kind? And what was rural beauty without main water? To have to draw your drinking water from a well that had a suspiciously river flavour, and hump your bath water by buckets from the river to the old sedge-roofed washhouse at the back of the house . . . she was right, Jennifer was right.

She stepped into the little ferry and began to pull frantically on the chain. The water felt cool, and there intruded into her irritation the thought that it would be nice to have a swim. By the time she had reached the other side and scrambled up the path through the tall reeds on the bank she was almost back to her normal way of thinking and she chided herself by saying, Now stop it and thank God for what you've got . . . for what we've all got. . . . Oh, she did, she did. She did thank God every day of her life for Heron Mill. Her only fear was that one day they would have to leave it. The fear rose in her now and almost checked her running. That day could be imminent. If anything happened to her father, that would be the finish. If he died, Heron Mill would die too, and they would have no home, with or without electricity. But Jennifer could have a home. Yes, that would be the one thing that would make Jennifer take Andrew. And when that happened she herself would have to do what she had always planned to go in such an emergency: take a job as a domestic—she was better at that than at anything else.

She was sprinting at an even greater pace now, thinking as she ran, Oh, dear God, don't let him die. . . . Like a child, her prayer was two-fold, for there was a great deal of personal benefit to be derived from its being answered. Much as she loved her father—and she did love him, not as a daughter loves a father but rather as a mother a wayward child—she loved the mill house equally, because in Heron Mill she had come to know her only home, she had come to feel a sense of security never

12

experienced before. Almost every day during the last six years she had told herself that all she wanted out of life was a home and security.

As she raced over the field towards the little wood she thought, I'll make for the top end and jump the dyke there. But as soon as the word dyke came on to the surface of her mind she shrank inwardly away from it and told herself, Don't take any chances. Go over the bridge at the Goose Pond—it'll only take you a few minutes more.

She might love the fen-land and the rivers with an almost passionate feeling, but she would never be able to bring herself even to look on the dykes with a favourable eye. These deep silt-filled slits in the black bog-like earth, which were as necessary to this underwater land as veins are to the body, had always filled her with a strange fear. Even in the daylight, when she forced herself to look down to the bottom of one she would shudder and imagine herself falling in and then trying to get out. An ordinary ditch had sloping sides, but those of most of the dykes were vertical. The thought of what would be the impossible task of trying to claw one's way up those soft silted banks always filled her with horror.

She was in the wood now and, her thoughts directing her route, she took the path to the left which would bring her to the Goose Pond, a name given to a broadening of the cut that was more in the nature of a miniature lake than a pond. The far side of the pond formed part of the boundary between Willow Wold Farm, Andrew's place, and the grounds of Thornby House, as also did the old, almost rotten wooden bridge that spanned the cut just beyond the pond.

For years now they had used the path through the woods in the Thornby grounds as a short-cut to Andrew's farm, for to go along the river bank on their own side, even as far as the Goose Pond, would have taken nearly three times as long owing to the winding nature of the river.

It is not really dark in the wood, not at this end anyway, for the trees were tall and well spaced. Towards the river, however, where the sapling willows made a denser undergrowth, it would be much darker. But as she knew the wood almost as well as she did every inch of the mill, the darkness presented no problem, and certainly no fear. For mile on top of mile in the fens it was possible to walk and not meet a soul. A chance encounter would nearly always be with someone known. Even in the holiday season, the hirers of the motor cruisers rarely ventured into the fens proper.

So the encounter was all the more startling when it took place.

She was nearing the edge of the wood and was a little out of breath. She also had a stitch in her side, when the thing loomed up in front of her. For a split second she imagined it was one of the cattle that had strayed from Andrew's land. This happened sometimes in spite of all the precautions Andrew took. But when she found herself pinioned in a grip as tight as a river grab, she let out a blood-curdling scream, at the same time lifting her foot and using it on her assailant. That her foot had found its aim on the man's shin became evident, for, emitting what sounded like a curse, he jerked his leg backwards.

"What the devil! What're you up to, eh?" She felt herself shaken like a rat. "Answer me! What've you been up to?"

"Take . . . take your hands off me."

There was a moment's silence, a moment during which she stopped struggling and the man's hands slackened their steely grip without actually releasing her. She could not see his face, she was held so close to him, but she knew that his jacket was of a rough tweed, also that he had been smoking, for she recognized the particular brand of tobacco—it was the same as her father used.

Strangely, this last thought seemed to calm her, and she was just going to demand, "Who are you?" for she was sure he was no one who lived within a wide radius of the fens, when she was dragged forward by the shoulder, and before she could protest effectively they were beyond the perimeter of the wood and in open land. And there for a long moment they both stood surveying each other.

The man before her was broadly built, thick-set she would have said if it had not been for his height, but it was his breadth that gave him the massive look, for he was under six foot. He was bare-headed and all his features stood out clearly in the moonlight. His cheek-bones were high, his nose thin, as were his lips. His chin was squarish and looked bony. In contrast to the blackness of his hair, his eyebrows were light and not bushy as one would have expected with the quantity of hair on his head and the bristle on his cheeks. They were narrow and finely curved and gave to the face a delicacy that every other feature on it contradicted bluntly. She could not see his eyes, for, although the eyebrows did nothing to shield them, the bone formation formed a deep cavity in which they now lay peering through narrowed slits at her.

Although she could not see his expression, her valuation of herself gave her his summing-up: a slip of a thing, of no height at all, with an oval-shaped face and a mouth much too big for it, a nice-ish enough nose, copper-coloured hair, too long to be smart and not long enough to be attractive, and eyes. . . . Like his own eyes, hers were screwed up and he would not be able to see them. Anyway, they changed from hazel to grey according to moods, and sometimes even to a dark sea green when she was angry. They could be that at this moment. She guessed the surprise on his face was caused by her sex, and this was proved when in the next moment he said,

"What are you up to, running mad like that? I thought you were . . . Who are you?"

Who was she? Who was he? was the question that should be asked. "What business is that of yours?" Her voice was high and still held a tremble of fear in it in spite of her outraged feelings.

"You're trespassing on my land. I think that should give me the right to call this incident my business."

"Your land?" She felt her eyes opening wide and her mouth following the same pattern. Then she brought it closed on a gulp and began, "You're . . .?"

"Yes, I am."

"Mr. Bradshaw?"

"Yes, that's correct."

"Well, I thought . . . I didn't know you were back . . . you've been coming back for . . . for years and never have."

"I've been in residence for three days."

The "in residence" sounded stuffy and on another occasion she would have laughed, but all she could think now was, Three days and we didn't know.

Then, she rarely went up that way near the house. Still, Andrew would have known. But Andrew had been away for the last three days at the cattle show.

She said, lamely now, "Oh, I'm sorry! I would have called if I had known."

"I don't expect visitors."

"Oh." She was slightly nonplussed, but too bewildered now to be annoyed, at his tone. "Very well." She nodded her head once before turning away.

"Wait. Who are you?"

"I'm Rosamund Morley from Heron's Mill."

She had merely hesitated in her walk and she was conscious now that he was following her.

"Where are you going at this time of night?"

"I'm going to Willow Wold Farm, Mr. Gordon's farm. I've got to get a doctor."

16

"Someone ill?" He was by her side now.

She kept her gaze directed ahead as she replied, "My father. He was smoking in bed and set the mattress alight."

"Is he badly burned?"

"He's not burned at all as far as I could see; the mattress didn't catch alight until we threw it out of the window . . . my sister and I. But he's overcome by smoke, we can't get him round."

"Wait." His hand came out and pulled her to a stop, and although she shrugged away from it she stopped and faced him.

"If the road to that particular farm is no better than it was twelve years ago and the doctor's got to find his way along here"—he stretched his hand downwards indicating the path—"it would be an hour, very likely two, before he gets here. Your . . . your father should have that smoke out of his lungs as soon as possible, if it hasn't already done the trick."

She shivered at the crudeness of his words.

"Where have you left him? In the air?"

"No. No, he's a big man, we couldn't move him. He's on the landing. I was going to get Andrew . . . Andrew Gordon to give us a hand."

"Come on." His voice sounded quiet now, ordinary, and as she looked at his retreating figure going back into the wood she called to him, "Are you a doctor?"

Now the voice changed again and the answer was flung back to her, "No, I'm not a doctor."

She hesitated, her hands moving tremulously near her mouth. Andrew wasn't a doctor either, he would have done no more than lift her father on to a bed; but had she reached Andrew's place she would have phoned for a doctor. What was more, she didn't like this man. Yet, nevertheless, if he could do anything for her father . . .

He was well ahead of her now and his voice sounded

17

indifferent, even as it said, "Well, anyway, I'll go and have a look at him."

Pulling herself as if out of a daze, she muttered aloud, "But I still must get the doctor." And she had turned about and taken half a dozen paces, when she was brought to a stop in her tracks. The next instant she was running frantically after the man. If he barged into the house—and barge he would, for that seemed to be part of his nature—Jennifer would have a fit, literally. She could almost hear her screaming. Jennifer had not the trust in the fens or its people that she herself had, that was why the doors had to be bolted at night, even although at times they never saw anyone for weeks on end, with the exception of Andrew and workers in the distant fields. At one time, when the Cut was kept clear, dinghies used to come up from the pleasure cruisers berthed on Brandon Creek, but not now, for the great clump of reeds breaking away from the bank had formed thick barriers here and there right up past the mill.

"Wait . . . wait a minute!" She was gasping hard as she came up to his side. "My . . . my sister would be taken by surprise if you went in . . . if you went in on your own. I must go with you, but . . . but I still must get the doctor."

"How long have you lived at the mill?"

She was trotting behind him now. "Six years."

"What became of the Talfords?"

"I don't really know. My uncle bought the place from an old couple—that's all I know."

"What do you do? Farm?"

"No, we haven't any land, just about an acre. Mr. Brown, he lives at yon side, he bought the land right up to the back of us. We . . . we make jewellery."

"What?" He paused in his walk and turned his head towards her.

She said with dignity now, "My father was a silversmith . . . still is."

"Oh . . . odd pursuit for this part of the globe."

"I don't see why it should appear so." Her voice was slightly huffy.

"I thought that kind of thing would have done better in a town."

"Whatever is sold in the shops has to be made . . . we make the jewellery." We did, she added ruefully to herself at this point.

They were out of the wood now and could see the gleam of the river. When they came to the ferry he looked down on the little red boat with scorn.

"Huh!" The sound was deprecating in itself, and the words that followed more so. "A new innovation. What's happened to the old punt?"

"How should I know?" She was snapping and hating herself for doing so, but this man's tone got her on the raw.

"It's likely lying somewhere upstream with its bottom out."

"Yes, that's exactly what happened to it."

"I thought you said you didn't know."

"I didn't know it had been used as the ferry; there's an old punt lying round the bend there, if that's what you mean."

"That would have lasted another thirty years with a bit of care. It was a fine-built punt; I used to see to it when I was a boy."

She did not ask, "Did you live here as a boy?" She knew from the little gossip she had heard about the owner of Thornbury House that he had been born here and had not left it until about twelve years ago.

When they reached the little boat landing he did not offer to help her out but climbed the bank and stood looking towards the mill. But when she reached his side he said, "It'll soon need stilts. The land must have sunk a foot since I saw it last. Have you had another step put on?"

"No." She walked past him. "The steps are the same as when we came. I'd better go in first and tell my sister." She ran up the five steep steps and into the hall, calling softly, "Jennifer! Jennifer!"

"Yes?" Jennifer came out of the room with the lamp in her hand. "You've never been there in this time. What . . ."

"Listen, I can't explain now. I've met Mr. Bradshaw from the House. He's back, he's coming to have a look at Dad."

"Mr. . . . But where?"

"Ssh! I'll tell you later."

As she turned the man stepped into the hall—just one step, for there he stopped. He was looking over her head, and she smiled a little cynically to herself. She knew what had halted him: Jennifer with her flaxen hair hanging over her shoulders, her frilly nightdress gushing out from beneath her three-quarter-length dressing-gown, and then her face, touchingly feminine in all its features. The wide blue eyes, the curved lips, the slightly uptilted nose and the thick creamy skin, and all this enhanced by lamplight. Definitely the Lady with the Lamp, Rosamund thought without any malice, for in spite of being the antithesis of her sister she loved her, and at this moment she was rather proud of her, for she was indeed having an effect on this brusque-mannered individual.

"This is Mr. Bradshaw. . . . My sister." The introduction was accompanied by rather an impatient movement of her hand, and then she asked, "Has he come round?"

"No."

Jennifer was still staring at the man as he followed Rosamund up the stairs.

As she crouched down beside her father, Rosamund looked across to where the visitor was kneeling on the other side, and she said, "He seems better now; he's breathing more deeply." She watched the man lift her father's lids, then put his ear to his chest. Afterwards he

20

raised his head slowly and stared into the older man's face.

"Is he . . . is he all right?"

"Yes, yes, I would say he's all right. At least, he will be after this sleep. Let me get him up." His voice had the effect of pushing her aside, and she got to her feet as he stooped with bended knees and, to her amazement, lifted the heavy form from the ground with no more effort than if it had been herself he was carrying.

"Show me his room."

"In here."

Rosamund snatched up the Tilley lantern from the table as she hastily made her way to her bedroom. Placing the lantern on the top of the chest, she flung back the rumpled bedclothes, then stood aside to make way for the man as he lowered her father on to the bed.

"He'll be all right. Cover him up."

Rosamund didn't like his tone at all. It was as if he were dismissing the whole thing as of little or no importance.

"I'm still going for the doctor."

"It will be a wasted journey and the doctor won't thank you."

"What d'you mean?" This question came from Jennifer, who was standing just inside the doorway now.

Mr. Bradshaw turned and surveyed her for a moment before answering, but her beauty apparently did not affect him enough to soften the brutality of his reply.

"Your father is in a drunken stupor."

Jennifer stared at him—too taken aback to make any denial. But Rosamund did. She said harshly, "No! He can't be."

"I'm afraid he can be, and is." He glanced over his shoulder at her.

"It was the smoke—he's not drunk."

The man now turned his look full on her where she stood by the head of the bed.

"Have it your own way, but he's not going to die from suffocation. He might have been a little affected by the smoke." He raised his finely arched brows now. "You seem surprised . . . don't you know whisky when you smell it?"

Did she know whisky when she smelt it? As far as she could remember back she had hated the smell of whisky. Yes, she knew whisky when she smelt it all right, for were they not imprisoned—Jennifer's word—in the mill on the fens because of precisely that . . . whisky. But she hadn't smelt any whisky from her father when they dragged him from his bed. For three months now he had never touched a drop, he hadn't been away from the place until yesterday. . . . Yesterday? But either she or Jennifer had been with him every minute they spent in Ely—he couldn't have got any yesterday. But he had. As much as she disliked the man standing opposite to her, she knew now that he was speaking the truth. His sense of smell was apparently more acute than her own, but, not only that, there were other signs that had told him that her father was in a drunken stupor. She had seen her father in stupors before, and she would have recognized the reason for this one immediately had it not been for the panic occasioned by the smoking bed. It had never struck her for a moment that he was drunk. As if the shame were her own, her head was bowing. Then, checking its downward movement, she jerked it upwards and, looking at the man before her, said, somewhat primly, "Thank you very much for your help."

As he stood returning her gaze without speaking she thought, He must think me an absolute fool, racing madly across the fens at midnight in search of a doctor for a drinking bout. At this moment she could have flayed herself for her stupidity in not realizing what the trouble was . . . what the stupor was.

The man turned from her and left the room without another word, and she felt as if she had been pushed bank against the wall, not by his hand but by his look, which said, "You little fool."

She looked now at Jennifer. Her sister was staring at her, her fingers stretched tightly over her cheek. She didn't speak until the front door banged, then the sound seemed to jerk the words from her mouth. "Oh, how awful, how humiliating. What possessed you to bring him here? If it had been Andrew it wouldn't have mattered. . . . Anyway, I don't believe him, I don't believe him. Father couldn't have got anything yesterday. Did you leave him?"

"Leave *him*?" Rosamund shook her head. "Do you think I would? I could ask you the same question. Did you?"

"No. No, of course I didn't. Only . . ."

"Only what?"

"He left me for a few minutes, in that café, when you went out to get the solder and things. He went to the cloakroom. . . . You know . . . you remember, it was round by that partition just near the door where we came in. Oh!" She put her hand over her mouth. "He must have slipped out. I remember now that shop next door. Groceries and wine-merchants. It would only take him a minute. . . . Oh, Rosie!"

"Well, it's done now. But why didn't we smell it? He did." She nodded as if the man was still in the room.

Rosamund now looked down on her father. He was breathing heavily and his face was flushed. Oh, why hadn't she guessed. She went slowly out of the room and across the landing to his room, and there, going down on to her hands and knees, she looked under the bed. But there was no sign of a bottle. Next she searched the wardrobe. Again no sign of a bottle of any kind. While she was doing this Jennifer was going through the chest-of-drawers.

"There's nothing here. Somehow I just can't believe it."

23

"Look, Rosie, he mightn't have gone to the shop, I'm just surmising that. Likely that man is just surmising what he said as well."

"He wasn't surmising, he knew all right. And so do we." Rosamund's tone was flat. "I would have had the gumption to realize it if it hadn't been for the panic over the fire. Well . . . there's nothing here, but he's hidden it somewhere. Wait!" She got a chair and, reaching to the top of the tallboy, she lifted the lid of what was used as a linen chest. Groping inside, she found what she was looking for, and not only one but four of them, four flat quarter-size whisky bottles.

"Four of them!" Jennifer looked at the bottles in disgust. "And he promised. Oh, what's the use?"

"Well, it's no use going on. As you say, what's the use?"

"But he promised."

"You should know by now that he's promised before. Come on, let's go downstairs and make a drink."

"I don't know how you can take it like that, so flatly, so calmly." Jennifer was talking at Rosamund as they went downstairs. "And then tomorrow morning he'll be full of remorse, disgusting remorse."

"And we'll forgive him as we've done before."

"I won't—I told him last time—I won't."

"Well, you'll have to marry Andrew and get out of it."

"Don't be flippant, Rosie."

Rosamund was entering the kitchen now and she turned almost fiercely on her sister. "Flippant? Flippant about this?"

"I'm sorry, but it was the way you were taking it."

"How do you want me to take it, tear my hair? I stopped tearing my hair years ago."

Rosamund sounded almost sixty-two, not twenty-two, as she made this statement, and at this moment she felt that she wasn't a girl, she had never been a girl, she had

24

always been a woman who had carried the burden of a weak, charming, drunken man. She went slowly towards the open fire that was still smouldering and threw on some pieces of wood. Then, going to the oil stove, she lit it, and when the flame was clear she put on the kettle. . . .

Jennifer was sitting at the table, her chin cupped in one hand, and Rosamund was sitting in the armchair to the side of the fireplace. Neither of them had spoken for some time. They were one with the silence of the house, the silence that these incidents created over the years. Always there came a time when, discussing their father, it was impossible to say anything more, the feeling was too intense. Rosamund remembered the first time this silence had fallen on them. Her mother was alive then. She had been nine and Jennifer eleven and her father was . . . off-colour. Her mother had said, "No, dear, don't go in to Daddy; he's got a very bad head, he's a bit off-colour." Jennifer had just returned from a dancing lesson and she had swung out of the room, banging the door, her ballet shoes in her hand. When Rosamund had gone after her into their bedroom to tell her what a pig she was, banging the door when Daddy had a headache, Jennifer had hissed at her, "Now don't you start else I'll slap your face. I'm sick of it, do you hear? Off-colour! I'm sick of the pretence. Off-colour! Why does Mammy keep on pretending? He's drunk, that's his off-colour, he's drunk."

"Oh, you're horrible. Oh, you're horrible, our Jennifer. Daddy isn't drunk."

"Don't be stupid." The tone was different now—quiet, hopeless.

She had sat down on the bed beside Jennifer and the silence had fallen upon them. She knew that Jennifer was right, there had been something funny about Daddy's headaches and . . . off-colours. Lots of things became clear in that moment, the main one being the reason why her mother's people would have nothing to do with them.

Her mother was a Monkton; even her father would say at times, "Never forget your mother is a Monkton . . . a somebody." The off-colour episodes too seemed in some way to be associated with this statement—"Your mother is a Monkton . . . a somebody." It was some years later before she realized why her father talked like this. He was not so much telling her that her mother was a well-born woman as blaming her mother for this fact. And yet he had loved her mother, who, in turn, had loved him. In spite of the "off-colour" there had remained between them a warm passion until the day her mother died. There had been rows, heart-breaking rows, which would nearly always be followed by a move to another town where her father was going to work for someone who would appreciate him. He was going to begin again and everything was going to be fine. And it should have been, for Henry Morley was a craftsman in silver. He had gone to work for the Monktons as a boy and trained under one of their finest craftsmen. Monktons was a renowned firm of jewellers and they were very good to the men who worked for them, the right men, and they realized that Henry Morley was a right man. He had the fingers for a setting, he had an eye for line and design. He was thirty and very young to put in charge of a new workshop, but the Monktons thought he was the man for the job; and with just the right amount of condescension Arnold Monkton, the head of the firm, told him about this decision. Three days later, when he was still walking on air, Henry Morley met Arnold Monkton's only daughter Jennifer for the first time—that is, to speak to. He had seen her from afar, but never had their glances met or their hands touched. When this did happen the impact on them both was like lightning and the outcome was as disastrous as if it had struck them, for Arnold Monkton did not play the forgiving father but let his daughter decide finally between himself and the upstart Morley.

The upstart Morley set out to show the old man, but

soon he was to find that the task was greater than he had anticipated in the first bright glow of love and ambition. He could find work, but only as a man in a workshop. Men who had worked up to high positions in this particular line kept their positions and did not favour anyone under them who thought they knew better than themselves. After five years working for three different firms, and striving to show them his worth, Henry Morley felt he needed fortifying. He had liked a drop now and again when he could afford it, and whisky was his drink.

In the sixth year of their marriage Jennifer presented him with a daughter. They called her after her mother. Two years later another girl was born. They called her Rosamund.

That night, long ago, when the silence had ended and she had sat on the bed and watched Jennifer almost tearing her ballet shoes to shreds because she would not need them any more, and listening to her talking, Rosamund was amazed to learn that they had lived in seven towns since she was born. She was also horrified to learn that that very day her father had again lost his job, and so for a time there would be no more ballet lessons. She had watched Jennifer throwing the torn shoe into the corner of the room before, in turn, flinging herself on to the bed and bursting into tears.

Perhaps it was at that precise moment that she had taken charge of the household, for she even imagined that she actually felt herself growing up, and she must have been right, for how else would she have decided there and then not to let her mother know that she was wise to the real nature of "off-colour".

When she was fourteen her mother died, and this disaster seemed to break up Henry Morley completely. Jennifer, who was sixteen at the time and left school, decided that she would go in for "rep", and she went in for it. At least she went after a job. It was as she was returning, full of the news that she had been accepted, that she was knocked down by a bus—entirely her own fault as it turned out. The joy at the prospect of being an actress must have blinded her, for she had walked straight under the on-coming vehicle. It was fortunate that she hadn't lost her leg, but she had lain in hospital for many months after the accident.

Henry Morley at this time became both a pitiable and despicable figure; it all depended on which of his two children was viewing him. To Rosamund he was pitiable, and to Jennifer he was despicable, and not without reason, for when she came out of hospital, able to walk only with the aid of sticks, it was to find that they had moved, yet once again, this time into two dingy basement rooms.

The crisis came the week that Rosamund herself left school. She had been three days in her first job helping in a day-nursery when Henry Morley went down with a cold that developed into double pneumonia. Added to this, Jennifer's handicap with her lame leg and the nervous state her condition had evoked made her useless in looking after anyone, even herself.

Such was the situation of the little family flitting from one town to another that they were virtually without friends. The doctor who was attending her father might have done something. He suggested the patient should go to the hospital, but Henry Morley's grandiose attitude, which he sustained even with a temperature of one hundred and three, convinced him that the daughters were very capable of nursing him and running the house. The doctor was not to know that there was only a matter of three pounds at that time in the house, and no prospect of that sum being added to in any way.

It was at two o'clock in the morning, while sitting by her father's bedside, that Rosamund wrote the letter to her uncle. She had only seen her mother's brother once and she was very small at the time. Her mother had dressed her and Jennifer in their best and taken them in a train right the way to London. They had gone into a big hotel and there she had met a man who looked surprisingly like her mother, and who had told her he was her Uncle Edward. She remembered him making her mother promise to keep in touch, and her mother saying that she would. But she hadn't. She had never heard her father speak of her Uncle Edward even when he was—off-colour. Yet at these times he would upbraid her grandfather, Arnold Monkton. She knew a lot about Arnold Monkton although she had never met him. And she came to realize that her father talked about her grandfather because he hated him, but he had not the same feelings towards her uncle. She sent the letter to the firm in London, and printed in a large girlish hand in the top left-hand corner of the envelope she wrote the word "Private". On the fifth day, the postman having passed the door yet once again and filled her with despair, she received an answer to the letter in person. Her mother's brother walked into the dingy, cold room, and from that day to this she always associated her Uncle Edward with God.

When her father was able to be moved he transported them all to decent rooms. Then one day he had asked her—not her father, nor her elder sister, but her—how she would like to live in a mill in the Fenlands of Cambridge. It appeared he had taken an old house with the idea of turning it into a week-end cottage for his family. How would she like it? Even without seeing it the mill on the fens took on a semblance of paradise.

But things did not go smoothly with regard to their taking up life in the mill, because Uncle Edward had a wife. Rosamund could never call her Aunt Anna, she thought of her as Uncle Edward's wife. On a visit, and unaccompanied by her husband, Anna Monkton intimated that it was a bit of a nuisance their going to live in the mill, for she had already gone to a great deal of trouble to furnish it, and a good many of her choicest pieces were there, and as there was virtually no road to the mill it had taken some time and not a little expense

for the house to be furnished at all. She had also intimated that they could not possibly exist there without a
boat on the main river.

Neither Rosamund nor Jennifer had liked their Uncle
Edward's wife, nor she them, and Rosamund particularly
feared her influence. This influence was made clear when
her uncle, rather shame-facedly, told her that he would
draw up a statement which would allow them to occupy
the mill during their father's life-time. He had laughingly
added that neither she nor Jennifer would find this any
hindrance, for doubtless they would soon be marrying.
Rosamund could almost hear his wife saying, "We're not
providing those two madams with a free gift."

What Rosamund was sure that her aunt didn't know
was that her Uncle Edward made her an allowance of
twenty pounds a month. The money was always sent to
her by registered letter. Twenty pounds a month meant
that they would be fed, and the mill would house them.

Henry Morley at this time was in no position, or state,
to make any protest, and he fell in with the arrangement
with the acceptance of a child, yet beneath this acceptance Rosamund was always aware of a war raging, a
private war, in which humiliation played a big part. For
there were weeks on end when he never earned a penny.

When they had finally come to the mill, Henry Morley
had been fired once again with the urge to . . . show
them. There was plenty of room here for him to have his
own workshop. He would start on a paying game, making imitation jewellery. All he wanted was a bench, a
furnace, a few tools, and the basic materials with which
to begin. By the time he had got these latter his enthusi-
asm had worn thin, but nevertheless he did begin, and as
time went on turned out some very presentable pieces.

But, as Rosamund found, it was one thing to make the
jewellery and quite another thing to sell it. After a great
deal of correspondence the only reliable opening for sales
was with a shop in Cambridge. The location was fortu-

nate but the demand was small. As the owner of the shop flatly stated, he could get machine-cut bangles and brooches that looked exactly like the pieces that had taken hours of painstaking eye-straining work to achieve and for half the price. Unfortunately, Rosamund knew that neither she herself nor Jennifer could ever hope to have the skill that was their father's natural gift, but Jennifer was better at it than herself. Nevertheless this did not prevent Jennifer from hating it, as she did the isolation in which she lived. Yet, as Rosamund sometimes thought when her patience was tried to breaking point, Jennifer knew the remedy. She could either marry Andrew or she could leave the mill tomorrow and get a job—if, metaphorically speaking, she would forget about her leg and stand on her own two feet. With her father it was different; physically he was incapable of manual work, and he was of an age now when it was too late for him to attempt anything else. There was, Rosamund knew, a strong link of weakness between father and daughter, and as long as they had her to depend on they would foster it, and because she loved them she rarely protested.

"I wonder why we didn't smell it?"

"What?" Rosamund turned towards Jennifer. "What did you say?"

"I said, why didn't we smell it?"

"Yes, why didn't we?"

"I've made the tea. You look miles away—what have you been thinking? Oh, Rosie. . . ." Jennifer suddenly jerked her chair towards Rosamund's, and, gripping her hand, she begged, "Think up something to get us away from here. I'll go mad if I stay here much longer."

"Now listen, don't start that again." Rosamund gave an impatient shake of her head. "You know you can get away from here tomorrow. Andrew's just waiting."

"That isn't getting away, and you know what I mean,

31

I'd only be moving a mile and a half across the fens if I married Andrew."

"He loves you; it would be different living like that."

"Well, I don't love him, not that way. I like him, I like him a lot. I even think I could love him and would marry him if he would get a job in the town."

Rosamund, rising impatiently to her feet and almost over-balancing Jennifer as she did so, cried, "Don't be so stupid, Jennifer. Andrew's a farmer, that's his livelihood and you should be jolly thankful he is offering you such a home. And look, I'm warning you, don't try him too far. He's quiet, but just you remember: still waters, you know."

"Rosie." Jennifer was leaning forward, hanging on to Rosamund's hand now, and her voice was low and entreating as she said, "If we could only get away for a while, just a while, say a month somewhere, abroad. Rosie . . . write to Uncle Edward and ask him—he'll do anything for you. And . . ."

The jerking of Rosamund's hand out of Jennifer's grasp stopped her flow of pleading. "I'll do no such thing—I couldn't."

"Very well." Jennifer pulled herself to her feet. "When Clifford comes next week I'll ask him myself."

"Jennifer, you won't. Don't spoil . . ."

"All right, all right, I won't. But, Rosie, I tell you I'll go mad if I have much more of this . . . this . . ." She spread her arms wide, and they not only encompassed the room but the whole wide stretch of fenland by which the mill was surrounded.

"Things will pan out."

"You're always saying that. . . . Rosie . . ." Jennifer was standing in front of Rosamund now and her head was bowed as she said, "If you marry Clifford you won't leave me here with father, will you?"

"Now, Jennifer, look." Rosamund swallowed. "There's no talk of Clifford and me. Look, don't get ideas into your head. Clifford comes here for two reasons: it's a place to make for upriver, and he knows we're lonely. He's . . . he's very like Uncle Edward; he's kind, but there's nothing . . . he's never . . ."

"You don't have to protest so much; he may never have said anything, but he's got the same look in his eyes as Andrew. He's in love with you. . . . Rosie, you . . . you won't be a fool and refuse him. You have no fixations about cousins marrying, have you?"

"Oh, Jennifer, don't take things so far. Please. . . . Come on to bed, I'm tired . . . we're both tired. It's been quite a night; we'll talk about this some other time."

As she made to pass Jennifer she was pulled to a halt. "But if he should, just say if he should, you'd do something about getting us away from here."

Rosamund gave a deep sigh. "Yes, yes, of course I would. Under these circumstances I would never leave you here, but I'm telling you they won't arise. Come on."

When they reached the landing Jennifer said, "But where are you going to sleep?"

"I'll take the couch in the attic."

"No, come in with me, there's plenty of room."

Rosamund, now looking up at Jennifer, smiled and put out her hand and patted her sister's arm affectionately as she said, "You know you hate us sleeping together; you love to sprawl, and I love the attic. Good night, I'll see you in the morning. I'll take the lantern. Good night."

"Good night, Rosie."

Before Rosamund took the narrow steep stairs to the attic she went into her father's room, and there she went systematically through his pockets. In a few minutes she had found what she was looking for—two pound notes and a quantity of silver. The whisky she guessed would have cost over two pounds, that would make up the five pounds he must have taken from the envelope a week ago. The five pounds was accompanying an order to Barratt & Company for a quantity of materials. Any letters to be posted were taken to the box that was nailed to a post on the bridge, three-quarters of a mile distance from the mill. The postman, when delivering the mail, picked up its counterpart. Her father had said to her casually that morning, "I feel like a stroll, I'll pick up the letters on my way. Is there anything to go?" He had known quite well there was something to go, as he also knew that yesterday they would be going into Ely. The craving for drink had made him as wily as a fox, but more stupid, or he would have considered the fact that he would be found out. But apparently to satisfy his craving he was willing to risk that. Sufficient unto the day was the evil thereof.

She replaced the money in his pocket, and as she threw the coat over the chair the sound of something hard striking the wood caused her to pick up the coat again, and when she drew forth a tin of lozenges she was given the reason why they hadn't smelt the whisky from his breath. The directions on the box: "Guaranteed to eradicate foul breath . . . plus the smell of spirits or beer." She returned the box to the pocket and went out of the room and up the ladder to the attic.

The attic was filled with a lot of old junk, which, silhouetted in the moonlight, gave a weird appearance to the room. That the faded couch against the window was often used as a bed was evident from the blankets folded neatly at its foot. Rosamund did not undress, nor sit on the couch, but she went to the window that reached from the sloping roof to the floor, and, curling her legs under her, she sat close to it, her head leaning against the framework, and as she looked out across the beloved land, across the river and the small wood, right to Thornby House, she did not think of the strange encounter with its master which had been the highlight of the last two hours; she thought of something that was of more importance to her, someone who was of more importance to her, and she sent her whisper out into the night towards the face of a young man which was now encompassing all the land, and she whispered to it, "Oh, Cliff, Cliff, ask me to marry you, please. Please, Cliff."

2

The antique grandfather clock with the painted dial that stood on the landing struck seven as Rosamund descended the ladder from the attic the following morning. She tiptoed quietly over the polished floor and down the bare oak staircase, for she did not want to waken either Jennifer or her father. She would light the fire, set the breakfast, then go for a swim. She always felt better after a swim in the morning, and on this particular morning she felt badly in need of a refresher. But when she opened the kitchen door she stopped in amazement, for there at the sink stood Jennifer.

"Surprised?"

"Surprised, baffled and bewildered." Rosamund looked at the table set for breakfast, at the fire burning brightly, at the kettle boiling on the hob, then, turning her eyes on her sister, she asked, with a twist to her lips, "You all right?"

"I couldn't sleep."

"That's not new, but it doesn't get you up at this time."

"Here, drink this cup of tea." As Jennifer handed Rosamund the tea they exchanged broad grins. Then as Rosamund seated herself at the table, Jennifer, going to the sink again and with her face completely turned away, said, "I did a lot of thinking when I went to bed last night, with the result that today I'm going hunting."

Rosamund slowly put her cup down on the table, and

she screwed her eyes up as she repeated, "Hunting? What d'you mean?"

"Just that. Do you know who we had in the house last night?"

"In the house?"

"Oh, don't be so dim, Rosie." Jennifer had swung round now and was facing her.

"You mean Mr. Bradshaw?"

"I mean Mr. Bradshaw . . . Mr. Michael Bradshaw."

"How do you know his Christian name?"

"Oh, don't ask such inane questions. What you should be asking me now is why I'm going hunting?"

"Well, why are you? Oh, no! Oh, Jennifer, not that—really!"

"Why not?"

"Why not, indeed. He was most rude, uncouth; bullish, like a fen tiger. I would say he is the father of all fen tigers."

"But an attractive one, you must admit."

"Don't be silly. He may be married, you know nothing about the man."

"Oh yes I do." Jennifer laughingly threw her head upwards, then, bending towards Rosamund, said, "You know, what bores me with Andrew is really his farm talk. He prattles on and on talking his particular kind of shop, and quite a bit of his prattling came back to me as I was thinking in the night. He's always kept on about the Thornby land not being cultivated, and the weed seeds flying over on to his celery fields. Mr. Brown and Arnold Partridge, from the Beck Farm, they keep on about it too. Andrew said they meant to do something, for there was valuable land lying waste, and if the owner wasn't going to make use of it, then he should sell it. Arnold Partridge even went as far as to make enquiries, and from information he gathered he found that our . . . Fen Tiger was a sort of rolling stone. He has been rolling ever since he left here when his father died. Andrew himself

36

remembers the father. He says he was as mean as dirt and that the two were always at each other's throats. And I remember now that Andrew had the impression that our Mr. Michael was going in for medicine."

"That's not right. I asked him last night if he was a doctor and he said he wasn't. But all this doesn't prove that he isn't married."

"I somehow think he isn't."

"Don't be silly. Just thinking he's not married is nothing to go on, merely wishful thinking."

"Is it? I remember the way he looked at me."

"Oh, Jennifer!" Rosamund put her hand to her head with an exaggerated gesture. "Don't be so childish. Honestly, you would think you were ten years younger than me instead of two years older. You of all people should know by now that the more married they are the more they look like that. The wolf glare becomes intensified when they're married." Rosamund suddenly threw her head back and let out a high laugh. "We've already stamped him Fen Tiger, bull, and wolf, and you are going hunting. Oh, Jennifer, stop being funny."

"I'm not being funny, I mean it. I'm going to pay him a visit today—quite casual like, as they say."

"I think you're brazen. Anyway, what can he offer you that Andrew can't in the way of material things? Whatever he does with his land will be in the nature of farming, you would still be stuck on the fens."

"Not with a man like that." Jennifer turned and looked out of the kitchen window. "That fellow wouldn't stay put; he'd want to travel, far, far, away. You know, Rosie, he seems like an answer to my prayer."

"All I can say is that you're talking as if you had a touch of the sun. And——" Rosamund was turning away in disgust from Jennifer when she swung round to her again and, stretching out her arm, wagged her finger at her, saying, "And don't forget that when you're making plans there are others who may be doing the same. What about our elegant Miss Janice Cooper? Their place is as near to him on the far side as we are. And she has one advantage over you. Besides being elegant, she knows how to farm. And then there's Doris . . ."

"Oh, shut up, Rosie. I wish I hadn't opened my mouth and just gone ahead and done what I want. At least, I thought you would see the funny side of it and not try to damp me down."

"I'm not trying to dampen you down, I'm not, and you know that." Rosamund's voice was now soft, even tender, and it sunk to a lower tone still as she ended, "But all of a sudden I feel afraid somehow."

"Afraid? What is there to be . . .?" Jennifer stopped talking at this point, and, turning her head quickly, she listened. Then with an impatient movement she said, "It's Father. Good Lord! Coming down at this time. Now for the remorse—I'm getting out."

"No, no; please, Jennifer, stay. Don't make him feel any worse than he is. You needn't speak to him, but don't walk out on him."

The next minute the door opened and Henry Morley entered.

He was a tall man and heavily built, with grey hair and a face that had at one time been handsome but which was now lined and sallow. One feature still remained to prove his past attraction: the eyes. They were a deep blue with a touch of humour in their depths. It was even evident at this moment, but of a slightly derisive quality. He did not look at Jennifer, who was standing near the window again, but towards Rosamund, and he asked, pointedly, "What happened? How did I come to be in your room?"

"Have a cup of tea first."

"Is it as bad as that?"

Rosamond returned her father's glance and she watched him rubbing the side of his face slowly with one hand. "You nearly set the house on fire."

38

"I nearly set . . . What d'you mean?"

"You must have dropped off to sleep when you were smoking. Jennifer luckily smelt the smoke in time."

"Oh Lor—r—d." The last word was dragged out. "But how did you get me into the other bed, I can't remember a thing."

Rosamund turned towards the fire and pressed the kettle into the red embers as she said, "We dragged you on to the landing, and as we couldn't get you round I went for Andrew." She paused here, and just as her father was about to speak again she put in quickly, "I ran into Mr. Bradshaw when I was going through the woods. He came back with me." Her voice was very low and her father's was even lower when he repeated, "Mr. Bradshaw? Who's Mr. Bradshaw?"

"Thornby House . . . the owner . . . he's back."

"And he came here and . . . and put me in your room?"

"Yes." Rosamund was passing him now, the tea-pot in her hand, going towards the table, and she went on, "You were suffering from the effects of the smoke and might have suffocated. That's why we had to get someone quick."

"But you weren't suffering from the effects of the smoke, you were drunk." Jennifer had swung round from the window and flung the bitter words at her father; and as they looked at each other she continued, "We never guessed, not this time, but he had to tell us. He had to tell us you were in a drunken stupor."

Rosamund wanted to turn on her sister and cry, "Shut up!" but she knew it would be of no use. If Jennifer didn't have her say now she would later—that was Jennifer's way. Rosamund, her eyes laden with compassion, were fixed on the man standing to the side of her. She watched him close his eyes, then slowly droop his head and cover his face with one hand as he murmured, "Oh no, no."

"Oh yes, yes."

39

At this Rosamund did go for her sister. "That's enough. You've said it, and once will do." She turned now and took her father's arm, and, pressing him into a seat, she said softly, "Come on, come on. It's no use taking it like that—it's done."

"I'll never be able to look the man in the face."

"No, but you can look us in the face after sneaking off and getting that stuff from Pratt's."

"Jennifer! Will you be quiet! If you don't I'll walk out and I'll stay out all day."

This threat, simple as it sounded, had the desired effect on Jennifer, for after tightly clamping her mouth she flung round and went out of the kitchen.

Henry Morley was now sitting with his elbow on his knee supporting his head in his hand, and blindly he groped out and caught Rosamund's arm as he muttered, "You know what I did?"

"Yes. Yes, I know. I would have found out sooner or later when the stuff didn't come, but I went through your pockets."

"I'm a swine."

"Yes, I know you are." She was standing close to him now, and as she put out her hand to him he clutched at it and pressed it against his cheek.

"God! What would I do without you, Rosie? No recriminations, no nagging. . . . It's been hell this last couple of weeks, Rosie. I planned it all, the day I took the letter to the post."

"Yes, I guessed you did. Well, it's done; don't let's talk about it any more." Her voice sounded matter-of-fact now. "But I won't be able to send for the stuff until next week. We've got to eat and the money isn't due until the twelfth, you know that."

"What can I say?"

"Nothing; don't say any more." She disengaged herself from his hand, and as she went to the table she said, "As

40

we cannot get on in the workshop until we get the stuff you'd better do a turn in the garden."

"Yes, Rosie. Yes, I'll do that."

Rosamund closed her eyes for a moment. His patheticness, his utter humility, cut her to the heart. She sometimes wished he would bluster, fight, even damn her to hell's flames for her interference, but he never did. Also, apart from anything else, she hated these occasions when she had to play the part of the stern mother, for it made her feel old, old inside. There had been times when she had cried out against it, saying, "It isn't fair, it isn't fair. Going on like this I'll be old before my time. Why can't Jennifer take the responsibility?" But that was before Clifford had started to come up the river every now and again in the boat. A look from Clifford told her that she was still young, merely twenty-two and . . . falling in love.

"What's he like, Rosie?"

"Who?"

"The fellow Bradshaw."

"Oh . . . bumptious, the great I am, lord of all I survey. HE-MAN, and detestable. The lot, I should say."

"He sounds pleasant."

"I shouldn't worry about him. I don't suppose for a minute you'll meet him. When I said I would have called if I had known the house was occupied, he told me quite bluntly that he didn't want visitors."

"He did?"

"Yes, he did."

"Well, in that case he'll keep his distance."

"Yes, I suppose so."

It came to Rosamund as she said this that if Jennifer carried out her threat he might be persuaded to lessen the distance between the houses. Jennifer was beautiful, and her limp, which she used as a whipping block on herself, might have a claim on the man's pity; it had on Andrew's. But then Michael Bradshaw was no Andrew.

41

He was as different from Andrew as a tiger from a deer. There she was again thinking of him, likening him to a fen tiger.

When she had first heard the term "fen tiger", she had really believed it was some form of animal until Andrew explained it was the name given to a type of fen man, now almost extinct, but not quite, for here and there a descendant of the type of man who had lived deep in the trackless, treacherous fenland, and who fought against the land being drained with cunning, craftiness, and even murder, were still to be found. They were independent, often surly, and could at times call up the fierceness of their forebears, those raw, dark, vicious men who fought the Dutch workmen of Cornelius Vermuyden who had come to reclaim the land from the water-logged wastes. The fenlands had at one time been so wild that the inhabitants had only made their appearances in the towns on festive occasions, perhaps merely once a year, when trouble nearly always ensued. Even in this day there were isolated incidents that made people say, "Oh, a fen tiger at it." And when this was said a picture was conjured up of a rough, crude individual with barely a skin covering the elemental urges that had at one time been allowed full sway. For many long years the people of the fens had been looked upon by the townsfolk as uncivilized—and not without reason, it must be admitted.

But all this talk of fen tigers had only succeeded in enhancing the charm of the flatland for Rosamund. That was until last night. But now she thought that if Michael Bradshaw was an example of a fen tiger there couldn't be a wide enough distance between the houses to suit her.

Yet her fragile, delicate-looking sister was set on hunting the tiger. . . .

3

It was half-past two when Jennifer, dressed in a cream linen dress that caught up the silvery gold of her hair where it hung from below the large brown straw hat, stepped into the ferry and pulled herself across the river. Rosamund, from the bank, watched her drying her hands carefully on an old towel she had taken with her, then hang it on the post of the landing. She watched her incline her head in a deep exaggeratedly gracious bow before taking the path through the fields that would, in about twenty minutes' time, bring her to Thornby House. When she disappeared from view around the fringe of the wood Rosamund turned slowly and walked across the bank and up the garden, mounted the steps and went into the house.

It was cool inside the house, dark, shining and cool. The curtains were drawn in the living-room. Rosamund always saw to it that the strong glare of the sun did not harm the patina of the furniture. She loved and cared for the furniture as if it was her own, and there was always with her a little dread of the day when she would, perhaps, have to leave these beautiful pieces. The Georgian desk with its gilt tooled moroccan top. Nearly all the furniture in this room was of the Georgian period. The bow-front chest, the chiffonier with raised back. Only the two splat-backed armchairs were Chippendale. She used to wonder why her aunt had brought these lovely pieces to this out-of-the-way place, until her father enlightened her. Anna Monkton apparently had been an auctioneer's daughter before she married Edward Monkton, and now, having almost unlimited cash at her disposal, she indulged in what was almost a mania with her, buying antique furniture and old china. Her father had added, and somewhat bitterly, that the pieces that filled this house were likely throw-outs compared to those she would have in her own home.

Rosamund could not see any of the pieces as throw-outs, and she guessed that neither did Anna Monkton. The mill had been intended as a week-end cottage, and she felt that her aunt had seen herself entertaining here in quiet and elegant style.

She now went to the desk standing to the side of the window, and, taking from one of its drawers an old note-book, she sat down and began to flick its pages. She had first started to scribble at the age of ten. When she was deeply troubled, or ecstatically happy, she experienced a driving desire to capture an impression of the emotion, and the only way to do this was to translate it into words. Her efforts at first were crude, and even now, twelve years later, she still looked upon them as frittling. She read the last piece she had written.

> River reed-pipe,
> Soft lined for water notes,
> Play the murmur of ripplets lapping the stalk
> Sent from the moorhen, as she floats,
> And the night-moth, as he alights to walk.
> River reed, play your music to the wind's time,
> And bend and sway in the dance,
> Nodding your head to the moon
> And stilling all river things in trance.

She had been lying on the bank in the shadow of the reeds above the Goose Pond when she had written that. The moon had turned the pond into a magic world. Beyond the pond the sedge looked like a forest of trees, and the patches of meadowsweet like spilt milk. Purple feathery fronds of tall grass patted her cheek, and she had felt happy. Clifford had been earlier in the day, and she had walked with him to the end of Heron Cut, where the boat was moored, and seen him sail away down the Brandon Creek.

The poem had seemed good in the eerie magic of the fen night, but not now—it needed altering, polishing. She suddenly closed the book with a small sharp thud and pushed it back into the drawer. She felt unsettled, nervous, as if something was going to happen. She wished Jennifer was back, she wished she had never gone; she was crazy. She stood in the hall and looked out through the open front door towards the river. Its appearance had changed completely in the last few minutes. The sun had disappeared and the sky was grey. The whole of the flatland before her was covered with a dull blue haze out of which the wood reared up black and stiff. It looked like a storm. Oh, she wished Jennifer was back. Still, she would be there by now and the storm would likely give her the opportunity she was seeking: further acquaintance with the fen tiger. It was odd, but she was thinking of the man under that name now.

She stood, uncertain what to do. She turned her gaze towards a narrow passage leading off to the right of the stairs. At the far end a door led into the room which they used as a work-room. Her father was in there now, trying to make atonement by doing new designs, work which he had promised "to get down to" as soon as possible. This meant, of course, when she had the money to send for the materials.

She looked out through the doorway again and asked herself what she would do. There were so many things she could do. There were the bedrooms, hers and Jennifer's—she had seen to her father's this morning. She could finish the curtains she had started last week. She could make some jam—she had picked enough currants yesterday—or do a bit of baking. It was rather hot for baking. She shook her head, but nevertheless went into the kitchen and commenced this last chore.

Her father liked blackcurrant tart; Jennifer liked sultana scones. She would make them both.

The rain started as she began to gather the cooking materials together. It came in large slow drops at first, then turned quickly into an obliterating sheet. A flash of lightning lit up the kitchen and a few seconds later Henry Morley opened the kitchen door.

"You all right?"

"Yes. Yes, of course. It's not forgetting to come down, is it?"

"Where's ... where's Jennifer?"

"She ... she went over to Andrew's."

"Oh, she'll be all right then. Nice smell." He smiled, and she returned his smile.

"Blackcurrant tart. As soon as it's done I'll bring you a slice."

"Good. Good." He nodded his head like a boy filled with anticipation of a beano, and when the door had closed on him Rosamund stood for a moment, her body quite still as she looked down at the table, and the pity and love in her cried, Poor soul, poor soul. He was, she knew, craving for a drink, yet, aiming to please her, he pretended he was dying for a piece of blackcurrant tart. If it had been in her nature to feel resentment on account of last night's business, his contrition would have melted it away.

It was as she was taking the tart out of the oven that she heard the scurrying in the hall, and as she opened the kitchen door she was nearly knocked backwards by Jennifer's entry.

"Good gracious! You're drenched! Why ..."

"Help me off with these things—I'm shivering."

Rosamund saw that Jennifer actually was shivering but as much with fury as with cold. "Wait, I'll get your dressing-gown." She dashed out of the kitchen and was

46

back within a minute or so, and as she helped to pull the soaked petticoat over Jennifer's head she didn't say, "What happened?" but "Why didn't you take shelter?"

"Where?" Jennifer turned her head and fixed her with angry eyes.

"Didn't you see him?"

"Yes, I saw him. . . . Oh yes, I saw him."

Again Rosamund refrained from putting a question, but said, "I'll get you a hot drink. Sit down."

It wasn't until Jennifer had finished her second cup of tea that she began to talk, and then only in short explosive bursts. "Of all the bumptious, self-satisfied, uncouth individuals. Who does he think he is, anyway? The Lord Almighty? . . . Back on the fens five minutes and acting as if he owned them. . . . As if he had drained them."

This unconscious touch of humour spurting from her sister's fury caused Rosamund to bite on her lip to prevent her from laughing outright. She asked quietly, "What did he do?"

"Nothing." Jennifer cast her eyes up to Rosamund, and repeated, "Nothing, just that . . . nothing."

"Nothing? Then what are you on about?"

Jennifer drew in a gulp of air, then let it out on a deep sigh, and this seemed to relax her somewhat, for her tone changed. Leaning back and looking up at Rosamund, she said, "When I tell you you'll see nothing in it, it won't sound the same. You had to be there and see his face and . . . and his attitude."

"What kind of an attitude? What d'you mean?" Even as Rosamund asked the question she knew quite well what kind of attitude Mr. Michael Bradshaw had taken.

"Well . . ." Jennifer threw out her two hands palm upwards as she said. "When I got to the house there wasn't a soul to be seen. I went along the side past the big drawing-room window—you know—I didn't intend to look, but when I realized there were no curtains up and that the room was empty, I did look, not only through the window but round about. The whole place looked as deserted as it always has done. I may as well admit that before I knocked at the door I had cold feet, I nearly turned and bolted, but when I heard someone inside I pulled the bell before thinking any further. The sound of it alone nearly scared me out of my wits — you've never heard anything like it, Rosie." She shook her head, before going on, "Then the door opened and there he was. He was in shirt-sleeves and was wearing breeches and wellington boots. They were thick with mud and him inside the house. Honestly, I didn't know what to say. I felt a bit of a fool and I stammered something about coming to thank him for his kindness last night. . . . Kindness, huh! He kept staring at me, staring and staring and not saying a word. Then just as he was going to speak something distracted his attention. It must have been a dog or something because he almost closed the door, but he kept saying, 'Go to Maggie. Go to Maggie. Go on now, go to Maggie.' Then the dog started to whine, not a doggy whine at all, as if it were in pain or something. It was really weird. And then he was bellowing at the top of his voice, 'Maggie! Maggie!' I heard someone scurrying across the hall and caught a fleeting glimpse of a fat old woman and a few seconds later he pulled the door open again."

"Did he apologize or explain or anything?"

"Apologize or explain! No, not him. He came outside and closed the door behind him and proceeded purposely to make me feel like a worm." She imitated his voice. "'There's no need for thanks, Miss Morley. Apart from lifting your father on to a bed I did nothing, except distress you and your sister.'"

"Well, he was quite right, you know."

"Yes, he might have been, but it was the way he said it, Rosie. He stood looking at me as if he knew everything I had been thinking since I met him last night. I . . . I felt as if I was practically naked. You've got no idea the effect he had on me."

"Well, it's your own fault, you can't say it isn't. It was you who decided to go hunting."

"Yes, I know, but don't rub it in. . . . Really, I must have been barmy to think I could fall for anyone like that. Give me Andrew any day in the week, at least he's human."

"Cheers. It's done some good, anyway."

"Oh, be quiet, Rosie, and stop laughing. You wouldn't have laughed if you had been there, I can tell you that. He hadn't been outside the door a couple of minutes before it started to rain, great drops, and naturally I thought he would ask me in. But oh no! He walked away from me along the drive and I could do nothing but follow him, and when we came to the gate that's half hanging off—you know the one—he lifted it aside and said, 'I'm afraid you're going to get wet if you don't hurry. . . .' "

"And then?"

"That's all—there was no 'and then' about it. I walked away like a little spanked child. I was furious and my leg stiffened and I knew that my limp was getting more pronounced with every step, and before I had gone many yards it began to pour, and the infuriating thing was I knew he was still standing watching me. I tell you, Rosie, he's an absolute beast. Fen tiger's right—he's uncivilized."

"He evidently doesn't want visitors. He told me straight out last night."

"But why? Anyway, when it was pouring like that he could have let me take shelter until it was over."

"Yes, he could have done that."

"Well, anyway, I hope he rots in his mansion. And he certainly will, for I can't see any of the men around here putting up with that attitude." She twisted round in her seat now and demanded once again of Rosamund, "*Who* does he think he is, anyway?"

"The master of Thornby House evidently . . . feudal lord. Come on, drink your tea up and forget about it, and if it fairs up this evening we'll saunter across to Andrew's."

Rosamund sighed again, and then she said, "It's funny he hasn't been over; he would be back early last evening."

"He runs a farm, don't forget."

"Yes, I know, but . . ."

"Here, butter that scone while it's hot." Rosamund handed her a plate, and Jennifer, getting to her feet and going to a cupboard near the window, took out the butter.

She was splitting the scone on the table before the window when her head came up with a quick jerk, and she put her face closer to the pane and peered through the rain. She had thought for a moment that she was seeing a little figure standing on the far bank of the river. She blinked her eyes, rubbed at the steam on the window and peered still more. Then excitedly she said, "Rosie! Rosie! Here a minute. Am I seeing things? Look, over there on the far bank."

"What is it?" Rosamund pressed her nose to the pane, screwed up her eyes, and after a short silence she exclaimed, "It's a child."

"A child? There are no children about here, not that size. The Browns are all over fourteen."

"It's a child, anyway." Rosamund was speaking as she turned hastily from the window.

When she opened the front door and stood on the top step she could see more clearly. It was a child . . . yet. She did not continue with her thinking but spoke over her shoulder to Jennifer. "Look! Hand me my coat." She kept her eyes on the child who was now pulling on the ferry chain.

"What are you going to do? Bring her across? There may be someone with her—perhaps some fisherman has come up this way."

50

"It doesn't look as if there's anyone with her, and there's no fishing up this cut, as you know."

As Jennifer helped Rosamund into her coat she asked, "Well, what are you going to do with her?"

"See where she's from first, or where she's going. She looks lost. And there's something . . ."

Again Rosamund checked her thinking. Instead she darted down the steps and across the garden, and slithered over the wet bank to the landing.

The boat had more than a few inches of water in the bottom, but she did not stop to bale out, and as she pulled on the chain and the craft came nearer to the far bank she cried to herself, Dear, dear God, poor little soul! And when she stepped up on to the landing and looked down on the pulpy, almost formless, rain-drenched Mongol child, her heart was filled with compassion. The tightly drawn lids from which peered the little eyes were blinking rapidly. The mouth hung open and formed a misshapen "o". The thick stubby tongue was lying on the bottom teeth; the fair, sparse hair, plastered to the skull, gave the head almost a bald appearance. The shoulders were humped, and the legs sticking out from beneath the short dress were like two pudding stumps. The child looked about nine, but it was difficult to tell its correct age.

Bending slightly forward, Rosamund said softly, "Are you lost?"

There was no answer, but the child continued to peer up through the narrow slits of her lids.

"Where is your mammy . . . or your daddy? Are they fishing?"

Still there was no answer, but the child, turning from Rosamund now, moved towards the boat and attempted to put her foot into it.

"Wait. Wait a minute." Rosamund peered about her through the rain, but there was no one to be seen. Well, she couldn't leave the child out in this, she'd better take her indoors. She lowered herself into the boat and, putting her hand out to the child, said, "Come on, careful now."

Cautiously the child stepped into the boat, and as she sat down on the wet seat she lifted her streaming face up to Rosamund and smiled. The effort succeeded in contorting the face still further and made Rosamund cry out desperately inside, the question that thousands of parents had asked before her: Why did God allow one of his creatures to be born like this?

When they reached the other side she lifted the child out of the boat, and, taking her by the hand, ran her gently towards the house. She came without protest as far as the top of the steps, but there she stopped. Tugging now at Rosamund, she released her hand and stood leaning half in and half out of the doorway, staring at Jennifer where she stood just inside the hall, her face expressing her feelings.

"Oh! Oh, Rosie, whose is she? Did you have to bring her in? What about her people?"

"You know as much as I do, and don't use that tone." Rosamund was muttering under her breath. Now she addressed herself to the child again, her voice calm and soft, saying, "Come in, dear, out of the rain. You can wait in here for Mammy." She put out her hand towards the child, but it shrank away now without looking at her, for its eyes were still fixed on Jennifer.

"Can't she talk?"

"I don't know." Rosamund straightened up, and, walking with a casual movement past Jennifer further into the hall, she murmured, "Take no notice, she'll come in on her own. You can bring me a piece of cake and some tea and perhaps I'll get her to . . ."

Rosamund's voice was cut off by a high weird scream and she turned in time to see the child flinging herself on Jennifer, hands clawing at her dressing-gown and her feet kicking at her legs. Jennifer, taken by surprise, had staggered back in fright, and now as Rosamund gripped the child around the body in an endeavour to pull her away, Jennifer too screamed. "Get her off me! Take her away! She's horrible! Dreadful! Look! Look at my hand —look what she's done."

At this moment the door from the studio opened and Henry Morley came hurrying in. "What is it? What's the matter?" He stopped dead at the sight of Rosamund kneeling on the floor holding a struggling misshapen child in her arms. "What on earth . . . who is she?"

"Look, look what she's done." Jennifer, now nearing hysteria, held out her bleeding hand.

"She did that?" Henry looked at Rosamund, and for reply she said, "Take Jennifer into the sitting-room, Father. Anywhere. Leave me alone for a while, please."

"She'll do the same to you. You should never have brought her in . . . the frightful creature. . . ."

"That frightful creature happens to be my daughter."

As if they had all been jerked by an electric shock they swung round to the doorway where stood Michael Bradshaw. At the sight of him the child gave a cry that was half grunt, half gurgle, and with a shambling gait ran to him. In one movement he had picked her up, and the child, with her arms tightly round his neck, straddling his hip in a way that spoke of long practice. Neither Henry Morley, Jennifer nor Rosamund spoke. There was nothing that any of them could find to say. To Rosamund it was as if he had dropped out of the sky like an avenging angel. Why hadn't they heard him pulling the ferry over? Likely because of their concentration on the child. This then was Jennifer's dog, this poor, poor child. She could still think of her as a poor, poor child although she had viciously attacked Jennifer, and at this moment her pity was not only for the child but for the father, this arrogant bombastic individual. No wonder he didn't want visitors, and no wonder, too, that he carried his pride high and used it as a shield.

Oddly enough it was Jennifer who was the first to recover, and in a shaking voice she protested as she held out her bleeding hand. "Well, look what she's done."

"That is entirely your own fault. My daughter happened to see you when you decided to visit us a short while ago, and apparently she didn't like what she saw and she must have come to tell you so."

"Now, now, look here, sir." As Henry Morley moved angrily forward Rosamund thrust out her hand and gripped his arm. After one long look at the older man Michael Bradshaw turned about and walked steadily down the steps to the river, the child bouncing on his hip as he went.

"But that's no way to go on. What's the matter with the man, anyway?"

Rosamund, pulling at her father's arm, said softly, "Look." She pointed to where Jennifer was going into the kitchen crying bitterly now. "Go and see to her, I'll be there in a minute. Go on, see to her."

As her father reluctantly turned away to do her bidding Rosamund made swiftly for the front door, and, hesitating for only a second, she ran down the steps towards the boat.

Michael Bradshaw had placed the child on the seat and had the chain in his hand ready to push off when she reached the landing. Without any preamble she knelt down on the soaked wood so that her face was almost level with his own and began rapidly: "I'm sorry; oh I am, I am. And please don't think it was meant. Jeannifer ... my sister ... she was frightened for a moment. She ... she hasn't been well lately. But we understand, we do, and we meant no ..."

"Save your breath, I know what you meant. Just let me repeat what I said last night: I want no visitors. And pass that on to your sister, will you?"

It was hard to believe that under this stiff steely countenance the man was feeling anything but bitterness and hurt pride. Yet she reasoned that were there nothing in him but pride the child would not have run to him so eagerly, nor been enveloped in his arms so tenderly. She hadn't liked this man last night, she didn't like him much more now, and yet, of a sudden, she was deeply sorry for him.

She stood up and turned away and walked stiffly through the rain. When she reached the hall door again she heard the rattle of the chain that told her they had reached the other bank, but she did not look round.

As she went into the kitchen Jennifer greeted her wildly with, "That's what it was. I thought it was a dog, or an animal, but it was her; it was . . . that!"

"Jennifer!" Rosamund's voice was like a sharp rap. "Don't call it 'that'. It's a child, a little girl. She can't help being as she is. And if you had a child like her, and you never know . . . no, you never know . . . how would you like someone to call it 'that dreadful creature'?"

Both her father and Jennifer were staring fixedly at her, and to her own dismay Rosamund knew that she was going to cry. She turned swiftly about and left the kitchen. Running up the stairs, she went into her own room and sat by her window, biting hard on her lip to prevent the tears coming.

The rain was easing off now and the sun was breaking through. Soon the whole of the fenlands would be a moving picture of sunlight, vapour steam, and glowing colour. This was the time she liked, sunlight after rain, the time that would bring a sense of peace weaving through her; but as she looked out over the fens now, she had the feeling that peace had been swept from her, that since last night and the coming of the owner of Thornby House on to her horizon peace had fled.

4

The following day was one of unrest for both Rosamund and Jennifer, partly because there was a sense of estrangement between them. Over the years they had had their tiffs, yet after sleeping on them they generally started the day clean, so to speak, but not after yesterday's scene. Rosamund knew that Jennifer had the idea that she should be whole-heartedly on her side, and she couldn't. If the man only had been in question, perhaps she might, but she could not condone her sister's attitude concerning the child.

And they had not, after all, last night strolled across to Andrew's. What had prevented them was not the tiff but the fact that the distance would be three times as long now that they couldn't take the short cut through the Thornby land. The road to Andrew's lay along the bank of the winding river, over the bridge near the Goose Pond, then through the cart tracks cutting the fields.

Usually it was Andrew who brought in the late mail, for he came by jeep to the bridge and walked along the riverbank; rarely if ever had he taken the cut across the Thornby land. But Andrew hadn't come last night, and it was well past his time for calling now. He usually came about six, and more often than not left early to do his last round. Rosamund knew that it was Andrew's absence that was puzzling Jennifer. Perhaps puzzling wasn't the right word, she could nearly say worrying her. This was the fifth day that Andrew hadn't put in an appearance. True he had been to the show, but he would have been back the night before last, and he rarely let two days pass without visiting them. At least that had been the pattern for the last two years. Before that it had been occasional calls, shyly dropping in.

And so, Rosamund said to Jennifer, in a rather terse voice, "I'm going to the bridge to see if there's any mail. Are you coming?"

Jennifer seemed to hesitate for a moment before replying, "No, it's too hot—my hip's been aching all day."

This statement usually elicited sympathy from Rosamund but not on this occasion. She merely said, "Very well," and went out.

As she walked along the bank of the cut she did not tonight take the usual pleasure in the activities of the river. The moorhens were darting back and forwards across the water leaving arrows of pale light in their wake, while their babies cluck-cluck-clucked in startled fright at her approach. A pair of grey, spectral-looking herons rose at intervals from the bank keeping their distance from her. One after the other they lifted themselves into the air with surprising grace for such large ungainly looking creatures. Rosamund was never surprised at the swans' graceful flight, but the herons didn't seem made for grace. As she watched them they brought her mind from its brooding for a moment and a familiar thought was resurrected once again, and she smiled as she said to herself, I couldn't live anywhere else, nowhere else in the world. The thought took her mind in a leap to Clifford and the coming week. It was the end of June and the vac. about to begin. It was his last year at the university, but he wouldn't know the results of his finals for a week or so. Yet by the sound of things he should get a first. This being so, it would mean a year, perhaps two, in America for further studies in Physics. Not for him a travelling scholarship, he would go to a university out there and stay for as long as was necessary, and then back to Cambridge with the position of lecturer to look forward to. She gave a little shiver, of delight or apprehension she didn't question, but she did question her place in this plan. Somewhere between the results of his finals and the end of the vac., when he would leave for America, she should know, for he was going to spend most of his vacation here on the river. He had already booked a small motor cruiser from Banhams in Cambridge. He would berth it where he always did, in the Brandon at the bottom of the Cut. Would it be early in the holidays or towards the end when he asked her? Well, that would all depend on . . . well, on opportunity, and . . . and other things. But ask her he would, for the only thing, she felt, that had prevented him so far from putting the question had been the intensity of the third-year work.

An arrow of wild ducks flying low brought her head up. Their wings flapping in their agitated fashion only emphasized their sure and purposeful flight. They were making, she knew, for the piece of marshland up the Brandon Creek where the water lay beyond the wash bank in shallow lakes, and the approach, except in the spring, was impossible, being too boggy for feet and not deep enough to take the more shallow-drafted boats. It was on that marshland, and from the top of the flood bank that she had first seen the two Canada geese. It was during her first spring on the fens, and the joy had stayed with her for days.

When she came to the Goose Pond a recently married pair of swans were training their young, cleaning their feathers diligently as an example to their eight cygnets, who waddled among the down discarded during their parents' toilet. The mother hissed at Rosamund as she passed and she spoke to it laughingly saying, "All right, all right, don't get flustered; surely you know me by now." There were a family of geese on the far side of the pond and they craned their necks and raised their voices in a protesting chorus at the sight of her. She crossed the bridge, being careful of the rotting plank in its middle, and stopped at the post to which was nailed the letter-box. . . . There was no letter in the box from Clifford or anyone else. Her disappointment was keen, but she told herself it was all part and parcel of this particular kind of day . . . of the last two days.

As she turned to make her way back over the bridge she glanced up the first of the long straight tracks that led to Andrew's place, and in the distance she made out a small shape almost obliterated by a cloud of dust. That was Andrew's jeep. She smiled to herself; it would be nice seeing Andrew, he was so sane, so easy to get on with. At one time she had wished that Andrew had taken a fancy to her instead of Jennifer, but it had only been a weak kind of wish.

As the jeep came nearer she thought with an inward chuckle, I'd like to bet Jennifer isn't so cool tonight. If yesterday's business did nothing else perhaps it's made her more appreciative of what she's been turning up her nose at.

The jeep was still quite a way off when Rosamund realized that Andrew wasn't alone, and when it pulled up opposite the bridge she only half answered his "Hello there, Rosie," for her whole attention was riveted on his companion. Why did the sight of Janice Hooper disturb her so much that she was almost unable to return her greeting? She looked at Andrew now. His colour was higher than usual and his voice sounded different, not Andrew's voice, as he said, "We're just off to Ely. Everything all right at the mill?"

"Yes . . . yes, Andrew."

"That's good."

"We . . . we thought you might be over last night."

"Well . . . yes, er . . . but I had one or two things to see to." He laughed. "You know what it's like after being away for a day or so."

"You should come to the shows, they are very interesting." Janice was leaning forward past Andrew to look at her. And Rosamund, returning the self-assured look, an-

59

swered coolly, "We are not farmers. There could be little interest at the show for us." It was the wrong thing to say in front of Andrew, and she could have bitten her tongue out.

Andrew straightened up and put his foot on the accelerator. The engine hummed and he turned his head once again towards Rosamund, saying quietly, "Well, I'll be seeing you. 'Bye, Rosie."

"Goodbye."

She watched the car bounce away. He hadn't mentioned Jennifer. . . . Janice Hooper had been to the show with him. She looked absolutely self-assured and possessive—yes, possessive, like a cat that had stolen the cream. Oh no, he couldn't be falling for her. Oh, Jennifer, poor Jennifer! She was still staring at the back of the retreating jeep when she saw it stop. She watched Andrew climbing down and come running back up the track towards her. He did not speak until he was quite close, and then his words were preceded by a gesture that showed his embarrassment. He rubbed his hand vigorously across his mouth, then took it up over his face and the top of his head before saying on a sheepish laugh, "Do something for me, will you, Rosie?"

"Yes. Yes, Andrew. What is it?"

"Well . . ." He looked at her under lowered brows. "Well, will you . . . will you tell Jennifer that you saw me with Janice?" He made a slight indication with his head towards the car.

"O . . . oh, Andrew!" The long-drawn-out "Oh" expressed only too clearly Rosamund's relief. She laughed now as she said again, "Oh, Andrew! You had me worried for a moment. But . . . but what about Janice? She likes you, Andrew." Rosamund nodded her head with superior wisdom. "I can tell."

"She likes lots of others." Andrew laughed selfconsciously. "Janice can take care of herself, I'm not worried about her."

"Anyway, I'd be careful. But I'll tell Jennifer. Oh yes, I'll tell Jennifer." She laughed again.

"I must be off now." He paused for a moment before turning and said rapidly and stiffly, "Jennifer's got to make up her mind one way or the other. I can't go on like this, Rosie. For two years now I've been asking her; four years I've been after her all together. I'll ask her once more and that'll be the last. But I want the answer to be yes, so I thought I'd give her . . . well, a bit of breathing space, so to speak. I've been too attentive; it's a mistake, Rosie."

"I'm sorry, Andrew, if she's hurt you."

"I must go, else Janice will take off in the jeep on her own—she's quite capable of doing it." He laughed now, and then became serious again. Looking down into Rosamund's upturned face, he said, "You're nice, Rosie. A fellow would know where he was with you."

"Oh, Andrew, that's no compliment." She screwed up her nose at him and shook her head. "It only means I'm dull."

"It doesn't, by gum! Many a time I've wished it had been you. But there it is. We're all a lot of fools, aren't we?"

"Oh, Andrew, go on, don't be silly." As she pushed him there came three loud blasts from the horn of the jeep and she laughed out loud as he pulled a comically frightened face before sprinting away down the road.

"Oh, Andrew!" Again she repeated the words. He was nice, was Andrew. Yes, perhaps she might have taken him if it had been herself he had first set his cap at. She didn't love Andrew, but that wasn't saying that she couldn't have grown to love him. Kindness and consideration went a long way with her, that's why she liked . . . she loved . . . Clifford. Clifford was kind and considerate.

But Jennifer must stop playing about, Andrew was no fool. As he said, he would ask her once more and that would be the last. Perhaps he was already thinking that

Janice Hooper would make a better farmer's wife than Jennifer, and undoubtedly he would be right.

She did not saunter as she returned home but walked briskly. But she stopped when she saw one lone magpie flying across the river. Closing her eyes quickly, she said, "Let there be two", and when she opened them she saw the partner. Good. She smiled to herself. One for bad luck, two for good. Things would work out all right for Jennifer. She was still laughing at her childish superstition when she reached the mill. . . .

"Janice Hooper? Andrew with Janice Hooper? Where were they going?"

"Ely, he said." Rosie's tone could not have been more casual.

"But where? The pictures?"

"Oh, I don't know; they were a bit late for the pictures —I just don't know."

"Stop being so damn smug. You know more than you're telling."

"How should I? I saw them in the jeep. He stopped and said 'Hello'. Janice Hooper said, 'Hello'. He asked how everybody was at the mill and that was that."

"Didn't he say when he was coming?" Jennifer's voice was quiet now.

"No. No, he didn't." At least this was the truth, anyway. "But I'll tell you one thing. I judged from what Janice Hooper said to me that she had been to the show with him."

"At the show?"

"Yes."

"Well, I suppose she always goes to cattle shows; she's a farmer's daughter, isn't she?"

"Yes, but I've never heard Andrew say he had been with her. Yet she made a point of putting it over. I thought it was rather odd."

When she saw the consternation on Jennifer's face she had to stop herself from going to her and putting her arms about her and blurting out Andrew's strategy. As Jennifer passed her, her limp definitely pronounced now, on her way out of the room, she could not resist putting out her hand and touching her. "It'll be all right," she said.

"Why should it? You always told me this would happen. You should feel very proud of your prophetic powers."

"Oh, Jennifer! Don't take it like that!"

"I'm not taking it like that. He's quite at liberty to go out with whom he likes. He's not tied to me, is he? I've refused him and that's that."

Jennifer seemed to gather pride from the fact that she had refused Andrew, and, withdrawing her arm from Rosamund's clasp, she went out of the room, but with her head at too high an angle.

Oh dear, oh dear, what next? Heavily Rosamund went through the hall and took up her favourite position on the top step outside the front door. What a day! What a twenty-four hours! Everybody was being as awkward as they could be. Her father to begin with, that man over there—she looked across the river—Jennifer, and now Andrew.

The twilight was merging the colours of the fens into a soft grey sameness. On the far bank, flitting from one solitary willow stalk to another, a kingfisher was aiming to pierce the opaqueness of the coming night with its brilliant flashes of blue, but on this occasion she had hardly noticed him, for her thinking was turned inwards. Then, as if some impish genie said, "There's still a little daylight left yet, let's give you one more thing to disturb you," she saw the child again.

She must have watched the bobbing head above the grass for some time before she realized it was attached to anything. Swifts and swallows flitted over the reeds in such profusion that the eye became used to the changing pattern, but when the head moved into the open ground on the bank above the ferry landing she was brought to her feet with a start and an exclamation of "No! Not again!"

She turned quickly and glanced into the hall before running down the steps. Jennifer was upstairs, thank goodness for that. She mustn't see this child again tonight; children like this needed getting used to. She could understand, in a way, her sister being repulsed. The reason she herself had not been repulsed was because, as she had told herself earlier, she had not Jennifer's artistic temperament.

She stood now on the boat landing and watched the child slithering down among the reeds at the water's edge. What was she to do? If she went across the river he might appear at any minute and then more fireworks. No, she would stay where she was. And she remained firm on this decision until she saw what the child intended to do. She was walking into the water in an attempt to cross the river, and she was dressed in what looked like her nightdress and slippers.

"Wait! Wait!" Rosamund scrambled into the boat and hauled frantically on the chain. It wasn't likely that the child could swim, and if she came a yard or so farther on she would be in a bed of silt in which she would sink in a matter of seconds.

She caught her just in time, and, leaning over the gunwale of the boat, she propelled her gently back, with her hand under her am. When she had moored the ferry she lifted the sodden child on to the landing and was rewarded with a smile that stretched the features into still wilder disorder. Then from the slack mouth there came a sound like a word.

"Wiv."

"Wiv?" Rosamund repeated the word softly.

The child, still smiling, pointed a thick finger towards the water and repeated, "Wiv."

"Wiv?" said Rosamond again. "Wiv . . . water . . . wiv . . . river."

The child made a laughing sound now. It was guttural and thick, but nevertheless it was a laughing sound. Again she said "Wiv" and pointed excitedly at the water. Her mouth was wide open, her tongue hung out over her teeth, and, to add to the distressing sight, her nose was running.

A thick rhythmic swishing sound brought the child's head flopping back on her shoulders now, and as she looked up to where two swans, coming from the direction of the Goose Pond, were flying to some point up the Cut away above the mill, she said, "Ca . . . Ca."

"Yes, Ca . . . swans." Rosamund said the word slowly, and as she repeated it she got to her feet. The swans were making for home, it was getting dark. What on earth was she going to do with this child? Should she take her across to the mill, then go and tell him? No, that would be silly, upsetting Jennifer again, and having him come barging over like a bull. And yet if she took her up to the house, what then? He would likely say that the child could have found her own way back. Gently now she drew her up the bank, and, bending down and pointing to the path between the high grass, she said slowly, "Go . . . go . . . to . . . Daddy." The child blinked at her, then calmly took her hand and moved forward.

Reluctantly Rosamund walked along the path. There was one thing at least evident: the child could understand, up to a point, what was said to it. With this in mind she drew her to a stop, and, pointing once more in the direction of the house that couldn't be seen from this distance because of the trees, she again spaced her words, "Go . . . home . . . Go . . . to . . . Daddy . . . Dark . . . getting dark." The pattern was repeated. The child looked up at her and, still keeping hold of her hand, moved forward.

Oh dear! Oh dear! She would have to go on and put up

with the reception she might get at the other end. There was one blessing: the night was warm and the child was not likely to catch her death of cold. Still, the quicker she had this wet nightdress off her, the better. She looked down at her now and said quietly, "Run?"

When she broke into a gentle trot the child began to gallop excitedly and would have fallen again and again, owing to the long nightdress, had not Rosamund steadied her, and at times pulled her upright. This latter action elicited the guttural laughter; evidently the child was enjoying it as she would a game.

When at last they came in sight of the house, Rosamund, drawing the child to her and pointing to the great grey building, said yet once again, "Go to Daddy." The child's reaction to this was as before. She moved forward, but still retained a grip on Rosamund's hand.

They walked round the broken gate and up the drive to the front door. When they reached it the child stood with her, waiting, as if she too were a stranger, a nervous stranger; and as she stood, uncertain what to do for the moment, the child, making a sudden strange noise in her throat, drew her attention to the far end of the house. There, standing as if transfixed, was Michael Bradshaw. He had a mattock in his hand and had evidently been rooting the ground. The child did not run to him but continued to make the noise as she held on to Rosamund's hand.

His approach was slow, and Rosamund could see that he was baffled, even taken completely off his guard for the moment. She said quietly, "I felt I had to bring her; she was down by the river again. She tried to cross." She watched him look down at the child. Then, stepping past her, he pushed open the front door and called, not loudly, but in a voice that showed his anger more than bellowing would have done, "Maggie! . . . Maggie!"

It was some seconds before there came the sound of a door opening, and then there shambled into view the fat old woman that Jennifer had described. She looked first at her master, and then at the child, and lastly at Rosamund, and she said, "Mother of God!"

"Mother of God, indeed. And she could at this minute be with the Mother of God for all you care, Maggie. I asked you, didn't I, to sit by her."

"I did, I did, Master Michael; honest to God, I did. She was in a sleep as deep as death itself when I left her. Don't you go for me like that, Master Michael; it's the truth, I'm tellin' you."

Rosamund watched the man making a great effort to control his temper, and now his voice was almost ordinary as he said, "Take her upstairs."

"Come away; come away, child." The old woman held out her hand, but the child would have none of it. Instead, she looked up at Rosamund, then, stepping over the threshold, attempted to pull her forward.

"No, not now." Her father was leaning down to her. "Tomorrow . . . tomorrow. Bed now. . . . Susie, go to bed now . . . chocolate. . . . Come."

The child would not be influenced by this inducement either, and Rosamund, feeling very uncomfortable, bent down and disengaged her hand. The result of this was that now her thigh was clutched by the two podgy arms.

"Now this is a state, isn't it? What's come over her, anyway?"

"Be quiet, Maggie." He turned from the old woman to the child again, and, bending down, he said sternly, "Susie . . . Susie . . . let go." His face was just below Rosamund's and she whispered to him, "Would you allow me to put her to bed?"

He straightened up and it was some seconds before he answered, and then it wasn't Rosamund to whom he spoke, but the old woman. "Get a light, Maggie," he said. Then, moving into the large, bare hall, he went on, "I'm getting a generator in, but it all takes time."

"Yes, yes." She was following him now, holding the child by the hand once again.

"The furniture hasn't arrived yet."

She did not make any comment on this; it was evident that the furniture hadn't arrived, the whole place was bare and smelt musty with years of disuse. He was going up the stairs, she walking behind him, but slowly, for the child's step faltered when she had to raise one foot any distance from the ground.

"In here."

They were in a small room. The only furniture was a camp bed and a chair. She watched him open a trunk, and after flipping garments here and there he took out a nightdress. Putting it across the camp bed, he said under his breath, "Be firm. When she's in bed tell her you'll be downstairs, she'll stay then."

"Very well."

Left alone with the child, she had a strong urge to sit down and cry, and for a number of conflicting reasons. Taking the nightdress off the child, she dried her with the top half of it, then slipped the dry garment over her head and pulled off her wet slippers, dried the podgy feet, and lifted her into the bed.

"There now." She stroked the hair back over the hard bony cranium. "Susie go to sleep?" She spoke her name as if she was in the habit of using it every night. Again she said, as she pressed the child gently down on to the pillow, "Susie go to sleep." And after looking at her for a long moment the child turned her face into the pillow and remained still. Rosamund stood and watched her for a time, then, remembering Michael Bradshaw's words, she said, "I'll be downstairs." When there was no movement from the bed she turned away and went out of the room, not closing the door but leaving it ajar.

When she reached the top of the broad, dusty stairway she saw down below her the figure of Michael Bradshaw. He was standing looking out of the long window to the right of the front door. As she descended the stair he turned slowly and came across the hall to meet her. What his exact feelings were at this moment she could not gauge, his face was giving nothing away. His voice sounded ordinary as he said, "I'm afraid I have nothing to offer you in the way of a drink, with the exception of tea, that is."

It was on the point of her tongue to say, "That's all right, I'll be making my way home now, if you don't mind, it's getting dark." This would have put her in charge of the situation and prevented her laying herself open to any sarcasm or rudeness which she still felt he might, at any moment, level at her. Instead, she heard herself saying, "Thank you very much, I would like a cup of tea."

He seemed slightly taken aback by her acceptance and he kept his eyes hard on her before turning away, saying, "Will you come this way then?" He pushed open a door at the far end of the hall that had once been covered with green baize, and stood aside, allowing her to go through.

The room into which he showed her was a kitchen, and she took in immediately that it was also the living-room. Partly covering the wide stone floor was an old carpet, and isolated in its middle stood a white deal table. Three plain wooden chairs stood near an old-fashioned delf rack that ran the whole length of one wall, and at each side of the antiquated open fireplace there was an old but comfortable-looking easy chair. It was to one of these he pointed, saying, "Will you sit down?"

As she made her way to the chair the old woman eased herself from a kneeling position in front of the large oven. "It's me back," she said. "And wouldn't this kind of contraption break anybody's back? Is it tea you're after?" She cast a glance towards the man, adding, "It's there on the hob."

"We want none of your stewed brew, Maggie. Make a fresh pot."

"Aw! Away with you!" Maggie now laughed towards Rosamund, and added, "The English don't know how to make tea. You got her to bed then?"

"Yes."

"It's strange how she's taken to you—isn't it?" The last part of the remark was addressed to her master, but he made no reply to it whatever. He was standing with his back to the delf rack, and Rosamund could now sense his unease. He was making an effort to be ordinary and it was evidently costing him something.

"Aye, she's taken to you." Maggie was carrying two plain thick white cups and saucers to the table. "And I've never known her do that since that time with O'Moore." Maggie cocked her head towards her master, and he gave a wry laugh. Then, looking towards Rosamund, he said, "I can assure you that is no compliment. O'Moore happened to be a sheep-dog."

"And a grand sheep-dog into the bargain; that dog had the intelligence far above the ordinary."

"It had indeed."

Rosamund smiled at his reply because Michael Bradshaw had answered Maggie in her own thick Irish twang.

"Aw, you were never the one to forget the body who did you down, were you, Master Michael?"

"No, I never was, Maggie." The voice still held the twang. But now he turned to Rosamund again and asked, "Have you ever been to Ireland?"

"No, I've never been there."

"Well, don't go, unless you want to be fleeced, befuddled and begoozled."

"Away with you! Where woud you have been without the Irish? Be fleeced, indeed. I've given you me whole life, that I have. . . ."

"Be quiet, Maggie."

There was a quick sternness in the words, but his tone altered as he turned yet again to Rosamund, saying, "The child took a fancy to this particular dog and would follow

70

it to its home. He was owned by one, Shane Bradley, the biggest scoundrel in the south of Ireland. . . ."

He had successfully diverted Maggie from personalities, for she cried now, "He wasn't that, he had to make a livin'. . . ."

"Make a living indeed!" Michael Bradshaw answered Maggie as he still looked at Rosamund. "He sold me O'Moore for five pounds. . . ."

"It was a grand dog."

"Yes, it was a grand dog indeed, as you said, a most intelligent dog." There was a twinkle in his eye now and he flung his large head upwards as he said, "Too intelligent. When you got him home you could chain him, bury him, chloroform him, but when you woke in the morning he would be gone, back to his master. Shane Bradley made a fine living in the summer, selling that dog to the gullible visitors. There is a tale that one fellow even got it across the border and it made its way back to home and Shane Bradley."

Rosamund was laughing now, laughing with an ease she would not have thought possible in the presence of . . . the Fen Tiger. She saw also that he was enjoying relating the story of how he had been done, and apart from him calling this Shane Bradley a rogue he gave her the feeling that he had liked this Shane Bradley. She was wondering how long he had lived in Ireland, when Maggie gave her the answer.

"Aw, you're always on about the Irish and Ireland, but don't forget it took the devil in hell to get you away from it after two years. If they hadn't said they were going to nab your land never a foot would you've put . . ."

"You jabber too much, Maggie. Where's that tea?"

"It's right here." Maggie handed a cup of black-looking liquid to Rosamund, another to her master.

"You take sugar?"

"No. No, thanks." She smiled at him, then sipped at the

71

tea. It was so strong and bitter that she didn't know how she was going to get through it.

"It's too strong for you?"

"Yes, yes, just a little." Again she was smiling at him. He took the cup from her hand and went to the sink and poured half of the tea away, then filled the cup with hot water. Handing it to her again, he asked, "Is that better?"

"Yes. Yes, thank you very much."

"Water spoiled, that is." Maggie was sitting at the other side of the fireplace, moving her body with a motion as if she were in a rocking-chair, and there now followed a space when not one of them spoke and the seconds began to beat loud in Rosamund's head. Michael Bradshaw was still leaning against the dresser, his look seeming to be turned deeply inwards. She forced herself to break the uncomfortable silence by saying, "It's almost dark, I'd better be making my way home."

Michael Bradshaw moved from the dresser and put his cup on the table. He did not speak as he went towards the door, but Maggie, stopping her rocking movement and raising her head, smiled at Rosamund as she said, "Aye well, we'll be seeing more of you if she's taken to you. There's not a doubt but we'll be seeing more of you."

Rosamund could make no reply to this, so all she said was, "Good night."

"Good night, Miss ... By the way, what's your name? I didn't hear it."

She did not say, as she usually did, "Rosamund Morley", but used the more familiar Rosie, "I'm Rosie Morley."

"Aw, it's a nice name, Rosie, comfortable like. Well, good night, Miss Rosie ... ma'am." She laughed as if she were enjoying a private joke.

Once again he stood aside as she went out of the front door. The courtesy seemed natural to him, yet up to an hour ago she would naver have coupled any kind of

72

courtesy with this man. He walked by her side to the gate without speaking and when they were on the field path he asked abruptly, "Do you like the fenland?"

"Yes, I love it."

"Well, you either love it or hate it, there are no half measures."

Yes, she knew this. Jennifer's attitude had taught her this much: you either loved or hated the fenland. They had walked on some distance before he spoke again, and then he began hesitantly, "I . . . I don't know what to say as regards the child. I . . . we can't keep her fastened up, and now she's found her way to the river"—he didn't add "and you"—"she'll make herself a nuisance."

"Oh no. Please, don't think that. If you don't mind her coming I certainly don't mind seeing her."

When he stopped she went a step ahead of him before she too halted, and as last night, they stood looking at each other. Then he said quietly, "Except Maggie and some of the Irish in Agnestown you're the only person who hasn't shown herself to be utterly repulsed by her."

Her throat felt tight, and she swallowed before saying, "You . . . you mustn't think like that. It's just that people are not used . . . They are apt to stare but they don't mean . . ."

"Were you used to seeing anyone like her?"

"Well . . . I worked for a short time in a day nursery"—she did not say three days—"and there was a child there, she was very like Susan."

In the gathering dusk she saw his cheek-bones moving, indicating the pressure on his jaws, and then, as if forcing the words through his teeth, he said, "It makes me mad, furious, raving, when I see the way they look at her."

"Has she been to school?" Rosamund's voice was very low. "A special school?"

"Yes, she's been to two. They are very good in their way, and they have an effect on some of them. Some of the children improve, but not Susan—they couldn't get through to her." He looked away from her and she knew he was seeing the child again when he said, "In the last place she was sitting there like a dumb animal in a cage. All the others were playing, laughing, talking their own particular jargon, but she was just sitting there, waiting, waiting for me." He turned round to her now, almost fiercely. "Somewhere there's a spark of intelligence, I know there is—it's only being able to get at it—she understands some things."

After a space of time during which she looked at him she said quietly, "Yes, yes, I'm sure you're right."

She watched him draw in a deep breath that pushed back the lapels of his coat, and then he said brusquely, "You know, you've been very kind . . . after the other night. My manner, I'm afraid, wasn't very tactful, or helpful. I'm sorry about that, but . . . but not about yesterday." His tone was rapid now. "Oh no. I could willingly murder anyone who calls her frightful . . . you understand?"

"Yes, yes, I understand."

They were staring at each other again when their glances were snapped apart by a far-away voice calling, "Rosie! Rosie! Ro . . . osie!"

"I'll have to go now. They didn't know I had come; they're wondering where I've got to. Good . . . good night."

"Good night."

She turned quickly from him and began to run. She found that she was running, not only to relieve Jennifer's mind, but to get away from something. What, she didn't rightly know. She only knew she was now running in a sort of panic and the desire was strong in her to escape, not only from the man whom she felt was still standing where she had left him, but away from the fens, the beloved fens, the deep, secret fens.

When she came to the boat landing Jennifer and her

father were on the far bank, and Jennifer cried across to her, "Where on earth have you been?"

She did not reply but dropped into the boat and pulled herself across the water.

Her father said, "I was worried when you weren't about—you didn't say you were going out."

She pulled herself up the bank before she said, "I had to take the child back, she was in the water."

What, again?" Jennifer's voice was high in her head. "You should have left her alone, you don't want to encourage her."

Rosamund's manner was so ferocious that it surprised even herself as she turned on Jennifer, crying, "And let the child drown, or be sucked into the mud! I was just to sit on the bank and watch it happen?"

"Well, you needn't bellow at me like that."

"Then don't be such a damned fool."

She stamped up to the house, her body quivering with a rage that was new and startling; it was as if she had touched the Fen Tiger and had become contaminated with his ferocity.

"Rosie, wait a minute." It was her father's voice, quiet and puzzled. She took no notice, but marched through the hall and upstairs and into her room. They could make their own supper, they could look after themselves. She had left the house for half an hour, and because she hadn't told them where she was going they were bawling the fens down. As her mind attacked them she knew that her attitude was merely a weapon warding off something else, something deeper, something that had made her run from the owner of Thornby House, the father of the Mongol child.

5

The following morning, when Jennifer brought her a cup of tea up to bed, Rosamund was embarrassed, ashamed, and a little amused at this gesture, and to cover her reaction she said, "I'm glad of this, I've got a splitting headache." She was looking down into the cup as Jennifer said quietly, "I'm sorry about last night, Rosie."

She glanced up swiftly at her sister and, putting her hand out, gripped her wrist as she said, "It's me who should say sorry. It wasn't a good day yesterday, was it? Tempers were running high on all sides. Let's hope today will be better."

"Father's made a good start anyway, he's been in the workshop since around six."

"No!"

"Yes, and he's off now down to the post."

"What on earth time is it?" She glanced at the clock on the table beside the bed. "Nine o'clock! *Nine* o'clock?"

Jennifer smiled broadly. "You slept on and we didn't disturb you."

"Lord!" Rosamund leant back and handed the empty cup to Jennifer. "Fancy me sleeping until this time, I've never done that before."

"I'll do your breakfast. Would you like it up here?"

"Good gracious no, I'm getting up. Thanks, all the same."

When Jennifer had left the room, she lay with her hands behind her head staring up at the ceiling. That's what crying yourself to sleep did. Slowly now she raised herself up into a sitting position. That was strange: she hadn't had her dream, not any part of it. She couldn't remember a night for years when she hadn't had her dream. It had become part of her life. She couldn't have been more surprised at this moment if she had realized that she had stopped breathing during her sleeping hours. Still, she swung her legs over the bed. The past two days had been unusual. You couldn't expect the pattern of life to remain the same.

As she entered the kitchen from the hall her father came in the back door.

"Hello, had a good sleep?" He smiled at her—he looked well this morning. As he handed her three letters she said, "Yes, I can't remember sleeping like that for years." She looked at the letters, two brown envelopes and one white. The white one brought a warm glow into her body and a sense of well-being. She did not open it but put it into the pocket of her dress.

Jennifer, aiming to be tactful this morning, made no comment on this, nor did she ask the obvious question, "Who is it from?"

It took quite some willpower on Rosamund's part to eat her breakfast, then help wash up and clear away, before she allowed herself to go into the mill proper. She had always felt it was a bit childish to keep Clifford's letters until she was sitting on the platform high above her world of the fens.

Once in the mill house she raced up the rickety stairs and was tearing at the envelope before she curled her legs under her to sit on the wooden floor.

"My Dear Rosamund." She was smiling at she began to read, but by the time she had turned over the single page of the letter her face had a stricken look, and when she came to the last words and read, "See you when I get back," she dropped her head until it met her uplifted hand.

She remained still for a moment, her fingers pressed on to her eyeballs in an effort to shut out the meaning of the letter. He would see her when he got back. His plans had

had to be changed. His mother thought that as he was going to America, anyway, it would be nice for them all to have the holidays there. His mother had a great desire to see her cousin in Washington as they hadn't met for years—"I'm disappointed, Rosamund, but will see you when I get back."

When would he get back? This was June, the holidays stretched through July and August and into September. And would he come back? Her aunt would see to that—she had smelt a rat. She was clever, was her aunt, wily. She could even hear her saying to Clifford in her high nasal voice, "Well, why go back to England? You'll only have a double journey. Why not stay on, now that you're here?"

With a sudden gesture Rosamund crushed the letter in her hand. She hated Clifford; he was weak, weak, like clay in his mother's hands. . . . No, no, she didn't hate him—Clifford was nice, kind and gentle. Clifford's trouble was that he wanted to please everybody, his mother included. She remembered again that she hadn't had her dream last night and the reminder brought with it a stab of fear and anxiety, and she spoke aloud, trying to quell her fears. "Why worry about that? Nothing has changed. You'll be here as long as father's here. . . . But it isn't only that, it isn't only the mill." And it wasn't only that, it wasn't only the mill. She wanted something else besides the mill. She wanted the kindness and the tenderness of Clifford.

She could see no beauty at the moment in the sun-drenched land below her and went slowly down the stairs and into the house.

As she entered the hall Jennifer was going into the workroom and she turned. "Well?" She was smiling with the question.

"Rosamund gave a little cough before saying, "Clifford's not coming, he's going to America. They're all going for their holidays."

78

"What! Oh, Rosie, that's Aunt Anna. But why can't he come and see you before he goes?"

"He'll be very busy; they'll be sailing soon."

"But all this must have been done in a hurry. Oh, Rosie"—Jennifer put out both her hands to her sister—"don't take it so hard."

"Don't be silly." Rosamund quickly warded off the sympathetic touch. "I told you, didn't I, that there was nothing. It was you who insisted."

"All right, have it your own way." Jennifer moved slowly back towards the workroom now, and just before she opened the door she turned her head and remarked, "It isn't the Morleys' week, is it—Andrew first, now Clifford."

Rosamund made no answer but went into the sitting-room, and there she began an onslaught on the furniture. At one point, when she was rubbing vigorously, deepening the already deep lustre on a small sofa table, she spoke to it, saying, "We must keep you at your antique best, mustn't we, for when Aunt Anna takes you over again."

Oh dear, dear, she hated to be like this. As Jennifer said, why couldn't Clifford have come and told her. Perhaps she would have understood then—at least she wouldn't have felt so hurt. The letter in her pocket was as cold and informal as if from a stranger. If he didn't care for her why had he kissed her on his last visit? They were at the end of the Cut—she was standing on the bank watching him as he started up the engine of the boat—and just before he let in the throttle he had jumped out of the boat on to the bank again, and before she knew what was happening she was in his arms and he was kissing her . . . once, twice, three times. And then he was down in the boat again. She had waved to him, not just with one hand but with her two high above her head, waved until he was lost to sight. And now he was off to America.

When the sting of tears came into the back of her eyes she chided herself sternly, saying, "No more of that, you've done enough crying lately. If this is the way things are to be there is nothing you can do about it but face up to it."

It was about half-past eleven when her father came hurrying from the garden into the kitchen, and, speaking below his breath as if his voice could be heard across the water, he said, "He's just taken it back."

"Taken it back? What do you mean?"

"The child."

"Was she . . . was she right here?"

"No, I first noticed him racing over the field. Then I saw him stoop and pick something up. It was the child."

Rosamund shook her head. "He's going to have his work cut out."

"A child like that should be in a home, you know, Rosie."

"She's been in a home, two homes. Apparently she pines. I should say she wants love. . . ." She stopped and added cynically to herself, "Don't we all?"

"She's not normal, Rosie." Her father's voice was slightly persuasive as if trying to convince her of something, and he went on, "She won't feel things like other children."

"Don't be silly." She had rounded on him angrily, and now she bit on her lip. "I'm sorry, but, Father, that type of child needs it more than the normal ones."

"Yes; well, perhaps you're right. You nearly always are. You're a wise little bird." When he came up to her and slipped his arm round her shoulders she wanted to cry at him, "Don't, don't." She wanted no sympathy today, no praise for being the little mother—she was tired of being the little mother, she was tired of playing the little mother to him and to Jennifer . . . and . . . and oh, she was tired of everything. . . .

By tea-time Michael Bradshaw had come within sight of the mill three times to Rosamund's knowledge alone, and the last time she had seen him carry the child back she had thought to herself, "This can't go on, he'll never get anything done at this rate."

It was as they sat having tea on the lawn in the shadow of the mill wall, out of the sun, that she said, and without leading up to the matter, "Tomorrow I will have the child across here."

"Oh no, Rosie, I just couldn't bear it." Jennifer held her cup of tea poised halfway to her lips.

"Well, don't you see that the man can't spend his days trying to stop her from coming here?"

"That's his business, I should think. Why doesn't he get someone to look after her?"

Rosamund opened her mouth to make a retort, then closed it again. Why? Yes, why? Jennifer was right there. The old woman Maggie was less than useless for running after a child. There came into her mind a picture of the bare house and the scantily furnished child's room and kitchen. She had seen such furniture before in the cheapest of cheap rented rooms. Why hadn't he waited for his furniture to come before opening up the house? Why had he bought that poor stuff? And why, if he was going to farm, was there no machinery, no man to help him? Why was he grubbing out roots with a mattock? Her thinking seemed to force the next words out of her mouth. "Well, if you can't tolerate her here I shall go over in the afternoons and see to her. Anyway, until we can get to work in the shop there's nothing to do."

Noticing her father's uneasy movement at this statement she could have bitten her tongue out for her tactlessness.

"It'll look very like pushing, won't it?"

"Oh, Jennifer——" Rosamund bestowed on her sister a knowing side-long glance and just prevented herself from saying, "You're the one to talk about pushing."

"Well, you go. Go ahead, do what you like, but he'll show you the door, you'll see."

"I don't think so."

"Well, try it."

"I have."

Jennifer was silent. "Did he ask you in last night?" It was her father asking the question.

"Yes, he did, and I put the child to bed and then he offered me a cup of tea."

She saw Jennifer's face darken and she understood her feeling at this moment. She herself would have felt much the same in her place, but she knew she would have refrained from making such a retort as now came from Jennifer.

"It's a case of love me, love my dog."

"Jennifer!" Rosamund was on her feet. "The child is not a dog, she's not an animal."

"Now, now, now. Both of you." Henry Morley spread his arms between them. "What's come over you all of a sudden? You've never been like this."

"Oh, I'm sorry . . . I'm sorry." Rosamund slumped down into the chair again, and after taking a deep breath she said quietly, "It's this heat, it's been unbearable all day. I think I'll go down to the pond after tea and have a swim . . . and cool off." She smiled apologetically across the table at her father and Jennifer. But it was her father only who returned the smile, saying now, "I'd do just that. I wouldn't mind going in myself, but it's such a long trudge down to that pond." He looked towards the river and added musingly, "It wouldn't be a bad idea if I were to clear a part up here. It mightn't be deep enough for swimming, but you could have a dip. Down near the bend there, say. What d'you think?" He looked at Rosamund for approval, and she was just about to answer when again she saw the child. She remained still, her eyes fixed across the river, and she knew that her father and Jennifer had followed her gaze.

The head came bobbing nearer through the high grass and when the child came into the clearing above the boat landing, she stood looking across at them, her mouth open, her face spread in a wide laugh. And the sound of her voice came across the water crying, "Wiv . . . wiv."

She was walking quickly across the lawn when Jennifer's voice came at her, low and pleading, "Don't bring her over here, please, Rosamund."

She did not reply in any way, but, getting into the boat and keeping her eyes fixed on the child in an effort to hold her attention, she pulled herself swiftly towards her.

When the ferry grated against the bank Susie was standing waiting for her, and when she stepped on to the landing the child put out her hand and without hesitation made her way up the bank again towards home.

With her shambling, erratic gait she kept ahead, intent on leading Rosamund back to the house, and a sad smile came to Rosamund's lips on the thought that indeed she had taken the place of O'Moore in the child's mind.

When they reached the broken gate the child did not lead her to the drive but along by a stone wall half obliterated with dead grass and shrub, and across what had once apparently been a garden. This was suggested to Rosamund by the hard stone path her feet found every now and again, and the rose bushes struggling for existence through the undergrowth. Then round to the back of the house and the stables and out-buildings, which, with the exception of a high barn-like structure, had been conquered by the luscious undergrowth.

It was as the child drew her nearer to the barn that she heard the voices. The unmistakable one of Michael Bradshaw was saying, "Yes, it'll take time as I'm mostly having to use sweat for money. I've got just about enough to get me started, that's if we live on the bread line. But I'll get going, never fear; if it's only to spite my dear neighbours I'll get going. Do you know that some of them were trying to get an order on the place." The voice was harsh.

"I heard something."

"Damned impertinence. I'd see them in hell before I'd let them have the land."

"How you going to manage without labour?"

"Oh, I'll manage."

"Are you going to furnish the place?"

"Furnish, huh! Furniture won't worry me. We have beds and a table, the bare necessities—they'll see us through until we get better. Maggie doesn't mind. There wasn't much else in her cottage."

"How have you managed all this time—I mean, have you had a job?"

"Oh yes, jobs in plenty." The voice was scornful. "Brawn pays better than brains these days. I even managed to save."

A laugh followed this, and then came the other voice . . . a pleasing voice, saying, "Well, you know, Mike, my week-ends are my own. I'll come and give you a hand any time. I'm not a stone's throw away, really."

As Rosamund pulled the child to a halt the two men came out of the barn, and she felt a wave of hot embarrassment flowing over her as they both stood looking at her without speaking.

"She . . . she was down by the river, I thought I'd better . . ." She broke off as Michael Bradshaw lowered his head for a moment, then, coming towards them, he looked down at the child before moving his gaze to Rosamund and saying heavily, "I've brought her back six times today."

"Yes, I know."

"She was here just a minute ago." It was the stranger speaking and they both looked at him, then Michael Bradshaw made the introduction.

"This is a friend of mine, Gerald Gibson . . . Miss Morley."

"How do you do?"

Rosamund looked up at the tall fair man. She guessed he was about the same age as Michael Bradshaw, yet he had that youthful, lively-looking air that made him appear younger, not thirty even. Her first thought was, He's good looking, and then, He seems rather nice.

"How do you do?" He was inclining his head towards her. "Morley? From Heron Mill?"

"Yes."

"Oh, I've heard about you. You took over after the Talfords left. It's years since I saw the mill. I used to go up there, up the Cut in a little dinghy, when I was a boy. Do you like it here?"

"I love it."

"That's odd. Most people have to be born here before they like it. I was born in Littleport, but we now live in Hockwold . . . you know, just beyond Wilton Bridge?"

"Yes, yes, I know it."

"Come." At the sound of Michael Bradshaw's curt syllable the child's hand was tugged from her own. As he made to walk away over the grass-strewn courtyard she said to him, "Would you like me to . . . to see to her?"

He stopped and seemed to consider for a moment. Then going on, he said, "No, no. We can't have that. Thank you, all the same."

The thanks sounded grudging, and she stood for a moment at a loss, feeling embarrassed because of the other man's presence. It was bad enough to be choked off without having an audience. She was on the point of looking at the man to say goodbye when an ear-splitting scream brought her round to the child again. With her two hands holding her father's, her body arched, she was almost in a sitting position in an endeavour to stop him from going on.

"Susie! Stop that!" He had her by the shoulders now and was shaking her gently. "Do you hear? Stop it!"

The screaming stopped and the child turned her face

85

towards Rosamund again. She was not crying, her eyes were quite dry, but in their opaque depths there was a wild look as if another scream was imminent. Michael Bradshaw's reactions came swiftly. With a lift of his arm he hoisted the child up and, apparently deaf to her now terrifying screams, he marched with her into the house.

"Don't be upset."

She looked up at this Gerald Gibson. His voice was kind, his eyes were kind. She said softly, "It's dreadful, awful."

"Yes, it appears worse when you're not used to it. He's used to it."

"Yes." She nodded her head in small quick jerks, then added, "I'd better go. Goodbye."

"Goodbye, and don't be upset."

She hurried away, and did not slow her pace until she was beyond the wood and out of sight of the house. Then she stopped and stood looking to where, in the far distance, her father and Jennifer still sat at the table on the lawn in the shadow of the wall. And as she stood she bit on her thumbnail. It was a long, long time since she had been so emotionally disturbed as to bite her nails. Even her father's lapses had ceased to make her bite her nails. She was thinking again, Poor soul, poor soul! but, strangely, the picture in her mind was that of the man, not of the child.

Jennifer did not want to go swimming in the pool. She had changed into an attractive print, one she had made herself, and she was waiting for Andrew coming.

Rosamund tossed up in her mind whether she would go for a swim or not. She did not relish her own company this evening; she wanted someone with her to take her mind off herself. There would be time enough to think about herself when she got to bed, for then there would be no chores, no diverting incidents connected with Thornby House and its occupants to prevent her from thinking of Clifford's letter, for she was fully aware that once she was alone the feeling that had been growing in her all day against Clifford would no longer hide itself under the term of disappointment but would take on its real name of resentment. Whenever she had thought about him today, and that had been often, she had resented so many things about him—the fact that he had been weak enough to fall in with his mother's wishes, that he had deliberately played on her emotions these past few months, that he had misled her with their last farewell. One could say, Well, what was a kiss, anyway? What were three rapid kisses in succession? The result of high spirits, payment for a happy day. Anything. . . . Anything apparently but a promise of marriage. So, to prevent her suffering her own company and self-questioning, she stayed with Jennifer. At least, she told herself, she would stay until Andrew arrived. But when by eight o'clock Andrew had not arrived and Jennifer's nerves were showing signs of strain, she felt she could no longer be with her sister without telling her of Andrew's strategy. So she made her way alone to the pool.

The pool was strangely deserted tonight, and there was not enough breeze to stir the reeds. When the long brown head of a bulrush wagged independently Rosamund guessed the cause to be a vole sitting on its hind legs, its back against the thick rush stem, as it nibbled off its supper from among the flat blades of grass. Nor were the swans and their cygnets to be seen; likely having gone down the Cut to the main river. For this Rosamund was thankful—she had too much knowledgeable respect for their tempers to get into the water when they were anywhere about.

She unbuttoned her overall dress and threw it on the grass near the large bath towel she had brought with her, then, going to a part of the bank which was firm with sunbaked blue clay, she let herself quietly down into the pool and began to swim. The water felt beautiful, wonderful. When she reached the middle of the pond she turned on her back and, paddling gently with her hands, lay staring up into the clear sky. A group of mallard, flying high, moved across her vision, and then a little barn owl. Then nothing for a long time. When she found herself reading her own thoughts in the endless sky space above her, she swung on to her stomach again and, thrashing out with the crawl stroke, made for the far bank.

"Enjoying it?"

She jerked her head upwards as Gerald Gibson's voice came to her, and, pressing down on her feet, trod water as she blinked upwards towards the bank.

"Are you enjoying it?"

"Yes. Yes, it's lovely."

"I wish I had thought about it—I had forgotten all about this pond."

"It's beautiful and cool."

"Come on out for a while." He was squatting on his hunkers and he patted the turf at his side.

Rosamund, still treading water, was on the point of saying, "My things are at the other side," when she thought, How stupid! It won't be the first time he's seen anyone in a bathing costume, and this one's almost old-fashioned enough to be Victorian. When she had swum the few yards to the bank he put down his hand to her, and with a lift and a pull she was on the grass, sitting by his side, laughing.

"I remember swimming in here when I was a boy. Every other week I came." He wiped the water from his wet hands. "You could get up the Cut in a boat then. The other week-end I made for the Railway Bridge. You know . . . right beyond Hockwold, near Brandon. Have you ever been up that part of the river?"

"No, I can't say I have."

"Oh, the fishing's marvellous up there. You can really

put your hand in the water, tickle 'em and pull 'em out. You can. Do you fish?"

"No. I've tried, but I find I haven't got the heart for it." She paused and laughed sheepishly. "I hate taking the hook out of their mouths."

"They don't feel it."

"That's what you think, but you're not the fish."

As they laughed together she thought of how different people were. Here she was, within a few seconds, laughing with this man she had met only that day, and then she had spoken to him not longer than a few minutes. He was the kind of man who made you feel at home right away. Easy, not like his friend. But then, he didn't look as if he had the responsibilities of his friend; he looked carefree. She felt so at ease with him that she could ask right away, "Have you had a nice day?"

"Yes. Well, sort of. I was pleased to see old Mike again." He turned his face full to her now. "He's got a hell of a life, hasn't he?" He seemed to take it for granted that she knew all about the owner of Thornby House.

Her face became straight as she said, "Well, I know very little about him . . . only the child . . ."

"That's what I mean, the child. He should put her away and keep her away."

She did not answer for a moment, and her voice was very quiet and perhaps held a note of censure as she said, "I don't think he'd find that easy to do. In fact, it would be more difficult than having her with him. He seems very fond of her."

"Fond of her? It's a mania. She's ruined his whole life."

Her eyes were wide as she looked at him.

"It's a fact, you know."

"Have you known him long?"

"Oh yes, since we were boys. We were at school together, then in the Army. Then he went to medical college and I into the Polytechnic. We roomed together for a time too, and then . . ."

89

"Yes?" She spoke quietly, waiting for him to go on, hoping he would go on.

"Well, he was in his second year when he met Camilla —she was his wife, you know. He went clean mad." He paused as he looked away from her across the pond. "It takes some people like that." Then on a little laugh he was looking at her again. "I'm glad I'm not that sort—too intense." He nodded his head at her, and as she looked at him, still thinking, He's nice, she also thought he would never be intense. Loveable, yes, but never intense. She heard herself say, "He didn't finish his studies then?" She knew that she wanted information about their neighbour and that this pleasing stranger was quite willing to give it to her without her doing much probing.

"No. No, he didn't. But, mind you, he realized that he had been mad almost before they were married a month. She was so unpredictable—a bit unbalanced, I'd say. But a man was apt to forget that when he was looking at her."

"She was beautiful then?"

"Yes, she was beautiful, and vivacious—auburn-haired and half-Spanish. She had her mother's colouring and her father's temperament. It was a very deceptive combination."

He shook his head as if remembering back; and as Rosamund looked at him, still thinking he was nice, she knew that here was a loquacious individual whom she had only to prompt to know all he knew about the master of Thornby House. She did nothing to resist the strong urge. "Is she dead?" she asked.

"Yes, drowned." He looked at her, nodding his head the while. "It's an awful thing to say but it was just as well, they would have driven each other round the bend if it had gone on much longer."

"When did she die?"

"Oh"—he screwed up his eyes thinking—"it must be around three years ago. I'd been staying with them; they

90

were in Spain at the time in a little village on the coast. The people were poor, everybody was poor, so they accepted the child. It was the child, of course, that was the trouble. But she didn't look so bad somehow among the pot-bellied urchins who ran about the shore. I had come upon them by chance, just sheer luck. I was touring at the time—hitch-hiking would be a better word. Mike was very much in need of real company, at least someone who talked his own language. I stayed with them nearly five weeks, but I hadn't been with them two days before I saw what a set-up it was. She loathed the child. She would have killed it, I think, if she'd got the chance." His face was sombre now as he inclined his head towards her. "This made Mike go the other way. He pitied the thing...."

"Oh, please!" Rosamund had screwed her face up and was now covering it with her hands. "I'm sorry, but I can't bear to hear her called ... a thing."

"Oh." Definitely the man was taken aback. Then he laughed. "I meant nothing. It was ... well ... after you're with her for a time you're apt to forget she's human."

"*No! No!*"

"I'm sorry. I can see that you look at her much in the same light as Mike himself does. But in his case I'm sure it was because Camilla hated her. The more she was against the child the more he was for her. And then she goes out one day swimming and that was that, it was all over. The strange thing was, I might have been with her, but I was too lazy that day to move. She was a strong swimmer, but she must have been caught in a current and sucked under. I left shortly after—I think Mike wanted to be on his own. He became ... well, rather strange. Things like that affect people."

"Did they never find her?"

"Yes. I wasn't there at the time, but her body was washed up. She's buried in the little cemetery. She's got

91

the distinction of being the only English woman to be buried there."

"It's all so very sad."

"Yes, I suppose it is. But there"—he laughed—"you've got no reason to feel sad. . . . Do you always come here swimming?"

"Yes, most days, weather permitting."

"I'll have to join you sometime."

She smiled and raised her eyebrows. "It's a long walk for a bathe, and the river's pretty wide near Wilton Bridge."

He laughed. "I'm coming to give Mike a hand at weekends. I'm going to get very, very dirty grubbing that ground."

She turned her head and looked at him seriously now, asking quickly, "What is he going to put the land to, beet and such?"

"No. No beet for him. He's going in for flowers. Chrysanthemums in particular, I think. Strange bloke, Mike; he's always been crazy about flowers. He aims to build greenhouses."

Yes, indeed, strange bloke, Mike. Who would have thought a man of his type and . . . manner would have had a feeling for flowers? It seemed rather ludicrous on the face of it. He had shown surprise when she had told him they did silver-smithing up at the mill. He growing flowers was more surprising still.

"But the Lord knows when he'll really get going." He shook his head.

"He's short of money?" But she already knew the answer.

"Short is right. He's got a bit but nothing like what is needed. He should be employing labour and machines to clear the place. But he's only got enough to carry him for six months or so. His old father was a bit of a swine, you know—he must have hated his guts. Mike always loathed this place, and now he can neither sell it nor let it. The

92

only thing he can do is live in it. He must have felt very loath to come back, for he's always said they could do what they liked with it. But some of the birds around here have been trying to get a compulsory order on the land. Well, anyway, here he is. And he's got some nice neighbours." The smile with which he accompanied this latter was a bit too pert and it brought Rosamund slowly to her feet. She was just about to take her leave of him with a laughing remark to match his own when she saw the subject of their conversation. Across Gerald Gibson's shoulder she saw in the distance Michael Bradshaw emerge from the wood. As she watched him hesitate for a second before coming on she was filled with an uneasiness and a desire to dive into the water. Her voice was quiet as she said, "Here's Mr. Bradshaw now."

"What? Oh!" Gerald turned and called a greeting to his friend. "Hello there." And as he drew nearer he shouted, "I'm still here. I met a water sprite."

Rosamond could not translate the expression on Michael Bradshaw's face as he came up to them; there was a blankness about it that could be hiding any type of emotion. It was, she supposed, a definite poker expression, but nevertheless it filled her with a vague unease. Whereas she certainly hadn't minded sitting next to Gerald Gibson in her bathing costume, under Michael Bradshaw's look she had the feeling that she was almost naked, and she wished heartily that she had her dress at this side. To cover her embarrassment and make light of the situation she laughed as she looked at Michael, saying, "I'm trespassing again."

"Yes, I see you are."

Oh dear, dear, he was utterly humourless. Surely he couldn't mean that he minded her being on this side of the pond? He hadn't minded her trespassing to take the child back. She felt the unfairness of the situation.

"Well"—she was looking him straight in the eye as she spoke—"I'd better get too my own side, I suppose."

He did not answer and she turned now and looked at Gerald Gibson, and she forced herself to smile amicably as she said, "Goodbye then."

"Goodbye. I'll be seeing you." His voice, high and pleasant, held perhaps just the faintest note of embarrassment. But his embarrassment was nothing compared to her own as she turned her back on them and entered the water. She felt hot with it, and with annoyance too, and this came out in her stroke, for her crawl sent the water spraying and she arrived at the other side somewhat exhausted. She suppressed the urge to turn round to see if they were still there, and, picking up her towel, she rubbed at her hair. Then she pulled her dress over her wet costume and slipped on her sandals. As she turned her face towards home, her name being called brought her around, not to look across the river but to the bridge and Andrew.

"Been havin' a dip?"

"Yes. I didn't hear the car."

"No, I walked over."

She waited for him to reach her side, and as she turned again she glanced casually across the pond. The two men were still standing on the far bank and looking towards her. Her sense of humour taking over, she laughed to herself. She had spoken to three men in a matter of minutes, two of them comparative strangers. This had never happened to her before. It would seem that the fenland was crowded with men.

"I'd like to bet that the burly one of those two is Bradshaw." Andrew had given a little jerk of his head in the direction of the pool.

"Right first time."

"Who's the other?"

"A friend of his, name of Gibson, from Hockwold. Do you know him?"

"I don't know him, but I know a Gibson, an elderly man, could be his father. By the way, are you on visiting

94

terms with his lordship?" Again Andrew indicated the pool.

"I wouldn't say visiting terms, Andrew. I bumped into him in the wood a few nights ago. I was dashing for you—father had set the bed alight."

Andrew stopped. "What happened?"

"Oh." Rosamund went on to relate her father's lapse, just touching lightly on it and also on the outcome of her meeting with Michael Bradshaw. But when she told him about the child, being Andrew he said, "Poor devil! He has his hands full, then. I'll drop in and see him some-time. Perhaps I can lend him something. You always want the loan of something when you're starting from scratch again."

Rosamund said nothing that would deter him from visiting Michael Bradshaw. The man's attitude to another man might be different altogether. Anyway, Jennifer would likely give him all the reasons why he shouldn't visit their neighbour.

"How's Jennifer?" Andrew kept his eyes looking straight ahead as he asked this question, and Rosamund too looked ahead as she answered, "I don't know how we'll find her now, but she looked rather beautiful when I left her a little over an hour ago. She had put on a new dress she had made—I think she was expecting a visitor." She glanced at him sideways and met his eyes now, and they laughed together.

"Do you think absence has made the heart grow fonder?"

"I would say it has, but don't overdo it, Andrew. She's . . ." She looked at him fully now as she said, "She's not very happy at present."

He nodded at her, and in silence they continued the journey to the house.

As Rosamund led the way up the steps she called, "Jennifer! Jennifer!" and when she received no answer she went into the sitting-room, only to find it empty, then into the kitchen, saying to Andrew as she passed him, "Sit down a minute, I'll get her." In the kitchen she found her father making a drink and asked immediately, "Where's Jennifer?"

"I . . . I think she went up to bed. She was a bit disturbed—in the huff, I think."

"Bed? But it's only nine and Andrew's here. Go and talk to him, Father, will you?"

"Yes, yes, I'll do that."

Rosamund, leaving the kitchen, went straight upstairs and into Jennifer's room.

Jennifer indeed was in bed and pretending to be sound asleep. Standing over her, Rosamund shook her by the shoulder and said, "Come on, you can't be asleep yet. Jennifer, listen to me. Andrew's here."

"Well, he knows his way back home."

"Don't be silly. Don't be a fool, Jennifer." Rosamund was hissing at Jennifer now, and Jennifer, swinging herself round in the bed and sitting up, hissed back at her. "A fool, am I? Yes, I know I am. I've sat there all night waiting for him. And last night, and the night before. I suppose Miss Hooper is otherwise engaged tonight or he wouldn't be here."

"Look." Rosamund was speaking patiently now, softly and patiently. "Get up, Jennifer, and get dressed. I'm telling you, don't let Andrew go away without seeing you. If you do you'll be sorry for it."

"Me be sorry? Why should I be sorry? I've been sitting here like a Victorian miss just waiting for him to condescend to come and see me. Ask yourself, has he ever come this late before?"

"He's been working."

"He's been working other nights but he could always find time to slip across. I'm not coming down, and you can tell him that."

"You'll be sorry, I'm telling you. You'll be sorry."

96

Jennifer's voice was calm now and had a cold ring to it. "I'll be sorry? What are you trying to tell me—that he's after somebody else and if I'm not careful they'll hook him? Well, let them go ahead. I'm not running after Andrew Gordon now, or ever."

On a burst of swift anger Rosamund leant towards her sister as she exclaimed, "No! But you could run after Mr. Bradshaw. Why, if you could do that, can't you pocket your pride and come downstairs for a minute?"

"You're an absolute pig. Go on, get out and leave me alone."

As Rosamund turned to go to the door Jennifer's voice hit her saying, "Now you can go and comfort dear, dear Andrew; you've always had a sneaking liking for him. Oh, I know."

Rosamund, filled with anger, turned and for a moment glared at Jennifer. Then, clamping her lips together, she swung round and out of the room.

She had no need to speak when she entered the sitting-room. Andrew, who was talking to her father, broke off for a moment to look at her, and then resumed the conversation—the house was not so large that voices would not carry downstairs. She left the room without speaking and went into the kitchen.

Five minutes later Andrew opened the kitchen door and, putting in his head, said, "I'll be off then, Rosie."

"I'm making some coffee, Andrew."

"Not for me, thanks all the same."

She walked to the front door with him, but she did not say anything.

Her father, embarrassed for Andrew, was standing behind them. "Good night, Andrew. Try to look in to-morrow."

Andrew made no reply to this but simply said, "Good night, Henry." Then, smiling somewhat sadly at Rosamund, he said, "Good night, Rosie."

"Good night, Andrew." She did not add to her father's invitation, "Come tomorrow." That would be up to Andrew. He was a quiet man, but a stubborn one. Jennifer was a fool.

6

It was seven long hot days later, and the occupants of the mill, each in his own individual way, was tasting unhappiness.

Henry Morley, because he couldn't get at his craft. The materials had been sent for but had not yet arrived, and Henry had found that there was only one thing that had the power to ease his craving, and that was work, even if the finished article was only an imitation of the real thing.

Jennifer was unhappy with an unhappiness that she wouldn't have believed possible, and all over Andrew Gordon. The old stick-in-the-mud Andrew Gordon. Andrew had not been near the place since a week tonight and she could not sleep for thinking of him . . . and Janice Hooper. And she was not a little puzzled at her own reactions, for she was now also full of self-condemnation over her casual treatment of Andrew during the past two years.

And then there was Rosamund. Clifford's defection had hurt her deeply, and she was filled with vague fears that she couldn't pin down but which were all mixed up with the insecurity of their lives. Their security was really no worse than it had been for years, yet in a strange way she felt that it was threatened. Life at the moment seemed very empty and purposeless. This had been added to by the fact that for the last five days she hadn't seen the child. The last twice she had taken her back from the other side of the river she had delivered her to Maggie, for Michael Bradshaw had been nowhere in sight. She just couldn't guess at what method he had adopted to keep the child in, but whatever he had done it had apparently succeeded.

She was in her room, actually on her hands and knees polishing the uneven wooden floor, when Jennifer came in. Her sister's voice was stiff and slightly sarcastic as she said, "You have a visitor."

"Me?"

"Yes. I would straighten your hair, you look a sight."

"Who is it?" Rosamund asked this question as she ran her fingers through the thick coppery tumbled mass of hair.

"Our neighbour, Mr. Michael Bradshaw." The name was given stress.

"Mr. . . . What does he want? Did he say he wanted to see me?"

"Well, he certainly didn't want to see me."

"Oh . . . oh." Rosamund pulled off her apron, and, again pushing her hands through her hair, went rather self-consciously past Jennifer.

"I've put him in the sitting-room."

Rosamund, glancing back at Jennifer, was on the point of saying, "What do you think he can want?" but decided against it and hurried on down the stairs.

When she entered the sitting-room Michael Bradshaw was standing facing the door as if waiting for her. She closed the door behind her and stood with her back to it for a moment before advancing towards him. She did not give him any formal greeting, but, rubbing her hands together and on a nervous laugh, said, "I'm very untidy, I was polishing the floor."

As he looked at her hands she felt that she wanted to push them quickly behind her back.

Reverting to formality, she said, "Won't you sit down?"

99

"No. . . . No, I can't stay. . . . Thank you. I've . . . I've come to ask you a favour."

"Yes?" She was looking straight up at him. "Is it the child?"

"Yes. She's been in bed for some days now with measles. Maggie does her best, but she's too old to keep running up and down stairs and I've . . . I've been tied for days and it can't go on, I've got to get the land cleared. I was wondering . . . if you could spare a few hours in the afternoon or"—he shook his head—"any time to relieve me. It would just be a temporary measure. I'm looking out for someone to take charge of her."

"I would be pleased to." She had not hesitated for a second. "My time's my own after lunch."

"It would only be for a short time until she's over this."

"That's all right. I wouldn't mind. . . ."

"I mean that; I don't . . ." His voice had risen a tone now. "I don't want to impose on your good nature. I am seriously looking for someone to take charge of her. The trouble is . . ." His chin jerked sideways and he went through the motion of pushing his cuff up and looking at his watch as he went on, "I couldn't afford to engage someone professional, say a nurse—not at present, anyway. May I ask if you know of anyone who would fit this bill around here?" He was looking at her again. "Someone not too old and yet not too young to be . . . to be afraid of her."

She shook her head and thought for a moment before she said, "I can't recall anyone to mind at present. The only young ones are the Brown children, and they are too young, they are still at school. I don't really know anyone in the villages, they are too far away."

"Yes, that's the trouble, the isolation."

"I can ask Andrew . . . Andrew Gordon. He comes in contact with quite a lot of people, he might know of someone."

"Thank you. I'd better state the facts whilst I'm on. I'm offering three pounds a week part time, or as much time as they will do for that amount, and I can't say for how long I'll be able to pay that, but I must have someone for the next few weeks; and again I'm not under the impression that that sum is going to entice anyone out this far. Still, there it is."

Every word he had said was indicative of the straits he was in, but no one would ever have guessed it from the tone of his voice. It was brusque, even haughty, as if he were proposing to make breath-taking terms, yet, strangely, she was not now adversely affected by his manner. She had the desire at this moment to pull him off his iron guard by saying, "Come on, what are we waiting for? Let's go!" Instead she said, "Will you have time to stay and have a drink, we usually have it about now?"

"No, thank you, I must get back."

He was moving towards the door now when he turned and, looking at her again, said, "I've told you before that I think you are very kind. I can only repeat it."

His words were so stiff, his manner so proper, she felt for a moment she would rather have him yelling at her, or being rude as he had been during their first two meetings. This kind of politeness she felt was entirely unnatural to him. He was the type of man who would laugh heartily, and curse heartily . . . and love grandly. She found herself blinking as she looked away from him. She said, "You are really doing me a favour. We're . . . we're very slack at present and there's nothing to fill one's time."

He was staring at her fixedly, and now he said in a more natural tone, "You want me to believe that, so I will."

"I'll be over shortly after lunch, about half-past one. Will that do?"

"Yes, that'll do." His hand was on the knob of the door and he was about to open it when his glance swept the room as he commented, "You have some lovely pieces

101

here; you are to be congratulated. It's something different from what it was in the Talfords' day."

She was looking towards the desk as she replied, "Yes, they are lovely pieces and they've created in me a passion for antiques, but . . ." She paused and turned her eyes to him again as she said quietly, "They are not ours, they don't belong to us." She was strangely happy that she was able to say this; it gave her a deep satisfaction to couple their own lot with his, and so she added, "Everything in this house belongs to my aunt. The property is my uncle's, and we can only stay here during my father's lifetime." She gave a little sigh here and finished on a wry smile. "My aunt will make short work of us once my father goes."

He seemed unable to answer her for a moment, and then a remarkably softening effect swept over his face. It couldn't be called a smile, it could be attributed rather to a slackening of tension in the muscles. "We could be practically what you call in the same boat," he said.

She nodded at him and smiled broadly.

"I'll see you this afternoon, then?"

"Yes, this afternoon."

They walked into the hall and out on to the steps, and there he turned and inclined his head towards her before running down the steps with a lightness of tread which was unusual in a man so heavily built.

Jennifer, coming out of the kitchen and joining her at the front door, looked to where he was stepping into the boat and she said, "He wants you to go and see to the child, doesn't he?"

"Were you listening?"

"No. But what else would bring him here? He can turn on the charm when he wants anything. It's a wonder I didn't slam the door in his face . . . I almost did."

Rosamund said nothing to this, and as she walked across the hall towards the stairs Jennifer was forced to ask, "What are you going to do?"

Rosamund, looking over her shoulder, now said, "Finish the floor."

"Don't be facetious, you know what I mean?"

"Well, since you've guessed so much, why can't you guess the rest?" Rosamund's voice was tart. "If you want to know, I'm going over after lunch today and every day until the child is better—she's got measles."

"Don't be a fool. You've never had it, you'll likely catch it."

"All right, I'll catch it." Rosamund was half-way up the stairs.

"It's contagious, you could bring it here."

"Well then, I won't bother coming back until she's over it, you can see to things."

"Rosie!"

"Oh, be quiet, Jennifer! And stop it." Rosamund had turned and was looking down towards Jennifer. "I'm tired of your grizzling and snapping. What you want to do is go over and see Andrew, swallow your pride and you'll feel better . . . and leave me alone. If I want to use my time by looking after the child, I'm quite at liberty to do so. My main work in this establishment is the cooking and chores, and I can get through those in the morning. Now . . . have you anything more to say before we close the matter finally?"

As Rosamund watched Jennifer's lips trembling she chided herself sternly for going for her, and she was about to apologize when Jennifer, jerking her head up, went hastily towards the workroom.

When she was once again on her knees polishing vigorously at the floor, she said to herself, It's the best thing that could have happened—it will take me out of the house; we're getting on each other's nerves.

For at least the sixth time Rosamund made an effort to leave the child's room, but was stopped yet once again by

103

her sitting up in bed and giving vent to an almost blood-curdling sound of protest.

Rosamund, pressing the hot head back on to the pillow, said patiently, "I'm coming back, I'm just going to make you a drink." She made the motion of lifting a cup to her mouth and repeated, "For Susie . . . a drink for Susie." But again there was the scream, so ear-splitting this time that she closed her eyes and screwed up her face against the sound. Then from the doorway came Michael Bradshaw's voice.

"I'm sorry. . . . I'm sorry you're having a time of it. I heard her over in the field." He advanced swiftly to the bed and, bending over the child, said sternly, "Susie! Listen!" He held up his finger before her eyes and again he said, "Listen! She's-not-going-to-leave-you-just-going-downstairs." He now pointed his finger rapidly towards the floor, then said quietly, "I'll stay with her until you get the drink."

Rosamund took an empty jug and glass from an up-turned box that served as a table to the side of the camp bed and hurried out of the room and downstairs.

In the kitchen Maggie greeted her with, "She won't leave you be, will she? God in heaven, but you're in for a time of it. An' I've had me share. She'd wear out the devil and all his imps, she would, that one. God help her. . . . You want more lemon water? . . . Give us the jug here. If that man doesn't get a break he'll end up as fey as the wee folks themselves. It's beyond human endurance, it is that."

Rosamund made no comment. She watched the old woman pour the boiling water on to the lemon, and when she was about to hand it to her Maggie paused in the operation, and, still holding on to the jug, she said, "She wasn't half as bad as this across the water. Two years I've had her over there. Of course I had only three bits of rooms and she was never out of our sight, and she could go out of the cottage door and play on the front

104

and still know you were near, but in this god-forsaken house of misery, upstairs must be like another world to her. I remember back to when I first came here, I was only a slip of a girl of thirteen and I was petrified at the whole set-up—the house, the land and everything."

She relinquished the jug, and Rosamund, saying no more than "Thanks, Maggie," left the room.

So Maggie had been here when she was a girl. That's what she had meant by saying the other night that she had brought him up. He must have taken the child to her in Ireland. As she climbed the stairs again she had a mental picture of a man travelling from one country to another, a child by the hand in search of what? . . . Peace? A solution to his problem? Rest? She didn't know.

At the bedroom door he was waiting for her, and he said under his breath, "If she falls off to sleep, leave her; don't stay in the room any longer than you've got to—it's very wearing."

She smiled quietly at him. "Don't worry, I don't mind. I don't find it wearing. When I do, I'll tell you."

As her smile broadened, he turned his eyes away and then his head. Looking across the wide bare landing, he said quietly, "If I believed in God I would be thinking at this moment that for every sore in life he provides a salve." When he brought his eyes back to her again she could not look at him. She turned from him and went into the room, and as she stared towards the child, sitting up once more, she put her hand to her throat. She was disturbed and the disturbance was creating a feeling not quite new to her. Again she wanted to run, run until there was a great distance between her and the owner of this house.

She set the jug on the box, then sat down on the side of the bed, and the child, as if at last reassured, flung herself back on the pillow and, turning on her side, stuck her thumb into her mouth and sucked on it avidly.

It was nearly half an hour later when Rosamund eased

105

herself cautiously from the bed. The child was sleeping now, breathing noisily through her mouth. Moving quietly to the window, she stood looking down on the tangle of growth that had once been the garden. To the right of her, in the distance she could see a gleam of silver appear where the sun was reflected for a second on a blade of steel. The effect occurred with rhythmic regularity. Michael Bradshaw was hacking at the stubble. Her eyes now swept the land around her, and she shook her head as if in dismay as she thought. How on earth will he ever get through this by hand? Taking in the land as far as the pond, and to the extent of Andrew's boundary on the south side, there must be at least a hundred acres. And when the winter came, what would he do? What would the three of them do in these cheerless, damp, high bare rooms? In this moment the problem was weighing on her as much as if it were her own.

She was turning from the window when the sight of a figure hurrying round the perimeter of the wood brought her eyes wide. That was her father. What could he be doing here? Had anything happened to Jennifer? She turned now swiftly but quietly and tiptoed past the bed and out of the room. She was still on her toes as she ran down the stairs. By the time she had crossed the wide hall and had opened the front door her father was nearing the end of the stone wall. She went down the drive towards the broken gate, and while she was still some distance from him she called, "Is there anything wrong?"

"No, no, don't worry." He came up to her breathing rather heavily. "It's this." He held out an air-mail letter. "Mr. Brown brought it over. He was in the village, in the post office, and Mrs. Yorke, thinking it might be important, asked him if he would send one of his girls down with it. It had just come in. It . . . it's from America."

As her father nodded down at the envelope in her hand she said to herself, Yes, it's from America, and she turned it over without opening it. She knew the writing;

106

it was from Clifford. He was already in America. Always she had opened Clifford's letters while sitting above the world on the platform at the top of the mill, but even if she had been at home she would not have kept this letter to read at the top of the mill. Moreover, she knew that her father was waiting for her to open it. As she looked at him he smiled and said softly, "Perhaps he's writing to ask you to go out there." Even as she said, "Oh, Father," she knew that something of the same thought had flashed through her own mind, and she also knew that it had brought her no excitement. She slit open the envelope and began to read, but she had not covered more than three lines when, jerking up her head, she gazed at her father and cried, "Uncle Edward. Oh no! Oh, Uncle Edward."

"What's happened?"

She looked down at the paper again. "He . . . he had a heart attack almost as soon as he left the plane." She was moaning aloud as she read the remainder of the short letter. When she had finished she handed it blindly to her father and turned away, cupping her face in her hands.

"My God! He was no age. Poor Edward. And he was a good man, was Edward. . . . Why? . . . Oh." He came to her side and put his arm around her shoulders. "Don't take it like that. There, there, don't worry. You were fond of him, weren't you? And he was the only one who ever did me a good turn in my life. Now, now. Oh, don't give way like that." He pulled her into his arms and patted her head. "You'll only upset yourself. . . . I wonder if they'll bring him back—for burial I mean. Not that we would be invited to go, not when she's in charge. Things will be different now."

The fear of the difference making itself felt, he released her, and, patting her shoulder, said, "Come on, away home."

It was some moments before Rosamund could speak, and then, drying her face, she muttered, "I . . . I'll have to go and tell him."

"Go on then, I'll wait here for you."

She went in the direction of the field and Michael Bradshaw, and some time before she reached him he straightened his back and looked towards her. Then, throwing his implement aside, he came quickly to her, saying, "What is it? What has she done?"

Rosamund closed her eyes and shook her head swiftly. "She . . . she's all right. My father has just been with a letter for me." The tears sprang from her eyes again as she ended, "My uncle, he's died. . . . They . . . they had just reached America."

He did not speak for some seconds, and then he offered no condolences but asked, "Was he the one who bought the mill?"

She nodded her head.

"Is it legally your father's?"

"What . . . what d'you say?" She raised her face to him.

"You said the other night it was your father's for his life-time. Is it in black and white?"

"Yes. Yes, I think my uncle saw to that, but . . . but it doesn't matter. He was quite young, and so nice, so nice. He was good to me."

"That wouldn't take . . ." He cut off his words roughly, then added, "You're going home?"

"Yes, my father's waiting."

"Will you . . . will you be going to see them—to the funeral? Are they likely to be bringing him back?"

"No, no, I don't suppose so."

"Will you be across tomorrow?"

"Yes, I'll be across tomorrow."

You could not blame him for worrying whether she would come and see to the child or not—he had not known her uncle—but at this moment she could not think of the child, or him, or anyone else. Her heart was sunk deep in the loss of the man she had coupled with God. "Goodbye."

108

"Goodbye."

He did not accompany her across the field, neither did he resume his work, but he stood watching her.

It was evening now and they were in the sitting-room. They had all been together for the last three hours, drawn close, as it were, by the shock of this tragedy, for tragedy it was in more ways than one. On the outside of her grief Rosamund was keenly aware that such security as they had enjoyed would be almost nil in the future. Even if her uncle had made a statement in black and white regarding the mill, there was the vital matter of the allowance.

It was the allowance that was on all their minds, and it was Jennifer who at last brought it into the open. She asked quietly, "Do you think the allowance will stop, Rosie?"

Rosamund let out a small sigh before she replied, "It's nearly sure to."

"Yes, as you say, it's nearly sure to." Henry Morley moved his head in pathetic little jerks. "She never knew anything about it, that's why it wasn't paid through the bank, always in registered notes. His life was difficult enough, poor blighter, without her knowing about that. But now . . ." He spread his hands wide and looked towards Rosamund.

Jennifer, too, was looking at her, and Rosamund had the desire to turn on them and cry, "Why look to me? There are solutions for both of you." She was tired, tired of thinking, of feeling responsible for them all. Jennifer, if she hadn't been a fool, could have been married to Andrew by now, and her father, with just that little bit more self-control, could have been in a decent job. She was sick of thinking for both of them. Again the feeling of youth had fled. She was no longer a girl of twenty-two. The future, their future, was piling the years on her once more, and she protested inside herself. Uncle Edward had been her one support both financially and morally, and now he was gone. She was sick of being leaned on. She herself wanted someone to lean on. Oh, she was tired of it all. Rising from her chair, she forced herself to say evenly, "I'm going to bed."

"Yes. We'll all go."

When they followed her from the sitting-room like lambs, still wanting to keep close to her, to the one who had always managed to work things out, she again had the desire to run. This time, strangely enough, across the river, towards Thornby House and . . . and . . . This last thought, checked at its telling point, carried her up the stairs to her room actually at a run, and, dropping on to the bed, she clutched tightly at the pillow before burying her face in it.

7

It seemed to Rosie that from the time she had heard of her uncle's death she had never been able to get away from the close proximity of Jennifer and her father. Even when she was over the river with the child so great was their need of her that she was drawn back to them almost against her will. Of late they had both become feverishly active in the work-room and always insisted on her being with them, although they knew that her skill was negligible in this line. She looked at them now, with their heads bent over the bench that her father had constructed roughly to the pattern of the first one he had worked at. There were the two semi-circular openings with the jeweller's "skin" attached to them. This skin, originally a receptacle for small particles of dropped filings of silver and gold and small tools, was merely a decoration in this instance, for never had her father been able to work with a piece of real silver since coming here. The space between him and Jennifer was strewn with wires of different thicknesses, and a conglomeration of imitation stones, all glass, ranging from deep rubies to emeralds. There was a hacksaw, and a range of tin-snips and shears. Pliers, both round-nosed and flat. Top-nippers and side-nippers. In fact most of the tools required for the work of a craftsman in silver. There were pieces of flat metal, showing variations of patterns done by puncher and hammer. But there was no plating vat, no gas to supply a blow-pipe. There was no modern electric drill. Henry Morley supplied the heat he needed from a furnace he had concocted in the old chimney breast of the room. But even with the lack of modern tools he could have turned out some fine work had the materials been forthcoming, and, if he hadn't been working against time, the time it takes to create a work of art in silver. Yet even now he couldn't hurry over what he termed in his own mind the trash. And Rosamund, knowing this, pitied him.

Her job in the process was to select and set the stones, and give the final burnish to the finished article before placing it on its bed of cotton wool in the little gilt cardboard box. As she now looked at the row of such boxes on the table before her she had a strong desire to jerk her hand and sweep them into the air. Her mind had been in a turmoil all morning, and not only this morning, but for days past, and she knew now that she had come to the point of decision. One of them had to go out to work, and obviously it would have to be her. There was absolutely no money in this work. She flicked a box with her finger. This kind of thing had to be mass-produced before you could make a profit, or you had to find a market that would pay well for good imitations, and that's what they hadn't been able to do. Yesterday she had wanted to shout at them both, "Let's drop this, it's like flogging a dead horse. We can go in the fields and help; the farmers want workers." But there lay the rub. The farmers did want workers, but could Jennifer with her limp last out a day walking, bent double most of the time, up and down the rows of beet or celery, or potatoes? And could her father, who had used his fingers as an artist all his life, numb his touch by grappling with the earth, even if he had the stamina to stand up to farm work? No. Then there was only herself left, and there was a job waiting for her. On this last thought she seemed to be pulled to her feet, and so quick was her movement that both her father and Jennifer looked at her enquiringly.

Wetting her lips, she stared back at them before saying, "I've had enough of this. You know it's no use, I'm going after a job."

"A job?" Her father's mouth was puckered with the word.

"Yes, I said a job."

"But you'll have three miles to walk to the bus unless you can get a lift." Jennifer was standing now and she added, "Unless he"—she jerked her head—"lets you cross his land."

"I won't be going to the bus. Mr. Bradshaw is looking for someone to see to the child, and he's offering three pounds a week. He went into Hockwold yesterday to interview a woman he had heard about. If he hasn't got her I'm going to take it on."

"Rosamund. . . . No. And three pounds a week!"

"All right! . . . I know it's practically nothing, but tell me what we're going to do for money. Profit on this——" She now actually did swipe the boxes aside. "We've sold so little recently it won't pay for bread and milk let alone anything else. Can you think of any other way? Or you, Father?" She was now glaring accusingly at her father, and as she saw his head droop she chided herself sternly, saying, Enough. Let up.

Her voice was quiet now as she went on, "There's no disgrace in taking such a job. Why should either of you

112

be so shocked? What's more, I'll be doing some good, I'll be useful. And it's only part-time."

"You're always useful, Rosie." Her father's words were scarcely above a whisper and they cut her to the heart. She watched him turn to his work again and Jennifer with him, then saying, "It'll be all right, you'll see," she went out of the room.

Going straight upstairs, she changed her dress, and, standing before the mirror, combed her hair. Then, pulling open the top drawer of the dressing-table, she took out some cosmetics and quickly made up her face. When she had finished she stood peering at herself in the mirror, and she jerked her chin at her reflection as she said: "You look worse. You look as old as you feel." When she gave herself the answer: "You couldn't possibly," she did not smile, she couldn't see the funny side of anything today.

She pulled open another drawer to take out a handkerchief and, seeing a number of letters stacked neatly one on top of the other, slammed the drawer closed again. In this moment she hated Clifford. Not a solitary word had she heard from him since the air-mail letter. She did not know whether her uncle had been buried in America or if they had brought him home.

She had written to her aunt, as had her father, at the Buckinghamshire address, but neither had received a reply. This silence too had told on her nerves. The fear was growing in her daily that in some way her aunt would undo any legal claim her father had to the mill.

There was no sun this morning. It was still very warm but dull and grey, and the weather matched her spirits. She had just lowered herself into the ferry when she saw Michael Bradshaw coming out of the wood.

"Is something wrong?" she called, before she reached him. "Is it Susie?"

"No, no." He shook his head vigorously.

"Oh!" She was standing in front of him, looking up at

113

him. He appeared different somehow. Then her eyes sweeping over him, she realized why. He was dressed in a grey lounge suit and was wearing a white shirt with a dark tie. He looked spruce, smart, townish.

"Were you coming to the house?" he asked.

"Yes." She lowered her eyes from his. "I was going to ask you something. It was about the job." She stopped. Her throat felt dry. Then, jerking her head up to him and looking him straight in the eye, she demanded: "Did you get that girl?"

"The girl? Oh." He shook his head. "No, the whole prospect frightened her. Me, the fens, the child, the lot."

She drew in a deep breath. "If it's still going, can I have it?" she asked bluntly. When she saw the laughter in his eyes she added brusquely, "It isn't funny."

"No, it isn't funny."

"We are on our beam ends, else I wouldn't ask. I don't want paying for looking after the child, but—but——"

"Rosie, Rosie"—he was speaking softly as if trying to penetrate through something—"of course, the job's yours. . . . *Yours*. You understand?"

It was the first time he had called her by her name, and she had the racing feeling inside again, wanting to run away, and yet . . . She stared at him. He was entirely different this morning. It wasn't only that he was dressed for town, there was something quite unusual about him. She said, "Do you want me to see to her until you come back?"

He nodded again. "That was part of the idea, but I came over to see you, Rosie. I've got news I wanted to tell you. I had a letter this morning. The gods have at last seen fit to be kind to me."

He straightened up, and he appeared more like the man to whom she had grown accustomed, as he said, "It would seem that we can only benefit, have our desires fulfilled, at the bitter expense of others. And yet"—he gave a little smile now—"I'm not going to be a hypocrite about this, Rosie. I didn't know him, I only met him once."

The smile became a laugh and he shook his head. "You don't know what I'm talking about, do you? Come on."

He took her arm almost roughly, turning her about, as he said, "I'd nearly forgotten. I've only an hour to get to Ely and catch the train. Do you think I'll manage it?"

She did not reply; she was slightly bewildered by his whole attitude and in some way apprehensive.

"Look, I'll give it to you briefly. Maggie will fill in the details, with many additions of her own, no doubt, before I get back. It's like this. My father had one brother older than himself and they fought like cat and dog—that's nothing to be surprised about, my father fought with everyone. I sometimes think I've inherited some of his qualities."

He turned his head and looked at her for confirmation of this, and when she gave it with a twinkle of her eye and a small nod of her head, he burst out laughing. He still had his hand on her arm as they walked along, Rosamund's amazement growing every minute.

"I only saw my uncle once," he went on, "and he liked me as little as my father liked me. Quite honestly, I don't believe I've thought of the old fellow half a dozen times over the years. I didn't even know he had married and had three children, two of them sons. This being so, it's understandable, I suppose, that he would make no provision against me inheriting. Who would have dreamed, least of all him, that they would all be wiped out together?"

Rosamund drew to a halt. "They were all killed together?" Her face expressed her horror.

"Yes. He had a yacht apparently. I don't know the ins and outs of it yet. I only know that the eldest son and the mother were found in the lifeboat . . . and they died shortly after."

"Oh, how terrible."

"Yes. Yes, it is." They were walking on again now. "When you let yourself think about it, it is terrible, and I should, I suppose, put on an armour of mourning, but I'm not a hypocrite. I'm sorry, naturally, but that's as far as I can go."

"When did it happen?"

"Five, six weeks ago, I think. In the meantime, they have been trying to trace my aunt's people, only to discover that she hasn't any. Apparently she was my uncle's ward when he married her—I don't know the facts yet."

They had reached the broken gate and he stopped. "I'll have to run now. You go and have a natter with Maggie. You'll hear all the family history, she knows it better than I do myself. Oh, Rosie——"

She found her shoulders gripped in his two big hands, and he whispered softly, "You're the sweetest thing this side of paradise, Rosie. Remind me to tell you that again when I get back." He touched her on the chin with his finger, a playful, caressing touch, and then he was gone.

She watched him running with great strides across the fields towards the main road, her heart thumping so loudly that it reverberated through her ears. When she turned to walk up the drive she realized she had the fingers of her two hands pressed tightly across her lips.

Did he—did he mean . . .? But there had been nothing, nothing to lead up to it, except gratitude for her being able to handle the child so well. By the time she reached the front door she was telling herself not to be silly, he was excited over coming into this money. In his position, she would have been drunk with excitement. That's how he was feeling. You couldn't hold him to anything he said, even if you wanted to. The sweetest thing . . . the sweetest thing this side of paradise. . . . It was just a saying. Translated, it could mean what had been said to her before, "Rosie, you're the kindest person on earth"; Rosie, you are the most understanding being in the world"; "Rosie, you are nice to know". But did they ever

116

say, "Rosie, you are beautiful"; "Rosie, I love you"; "Rosie, will you marry me?" No, no, they scuttered off to America and sent a weak apology for their absence. But Michael Bradshaw was no Clifford Monkton, there was no weakness in him. What he said he would mean. And yet . . . There were so many "and yets". There definitely were weaknesses in Michael Bradshaw and she had proof of them, and under the intoxication of an inheritance could he be held responsible for anything he might say?

She did not enter the house, but turned and looked across the fen. To the right of her for a space that covered about an acre, the earth was black. It had taken him over a month to clear that part. Suddenly she wished that things need not change, that he would go on clearing the land, by hand, that there would be no swift alteration. Jennifer's words came back to her. "He's not the one to stay put, he would travel."

Yes, when he had money he would certainly travel. He hated the fens, he had said so. She was filled now with a strange sadness. She would never, she knew, love any part of the earth as she did the fens. This was her land. She had adopted it with the same tenacity as would a nature-starved woman take a child into her life. He hated the fens and she loved them. He would go and she would stay.

The child had played quietly, but always in sight of Rosamund until shortly after two o'clock, when she fell asleep, and Rosamund took advantage of this to run back to the mill and tell her father and Jennifer that she would be staying up at the house until Michael Bradshaw returned. She did not pass on anything that he had told her. Her reticence on his occasion centred around Jennifer. If she knew the Fen Tiger was now a man of means it would not increase her liking for him but, under the present circumstances, would likely make her feel that she had been deprived yet once again of something

117

worth while. What she did tell them was that she had got the job, and to this neither of them said a word.

It was shortly before Rosamund was going to put Susie to bed that she heard her scream, and, rushing to the front door, she saw the child standing beyond the broken gate looking towards the wood. Her mouth was wide, and her body rigid.

"Susie! Susie! Stop it! Stop it! Do you hear? Stop it this minute!" Holding the child by the shoulders, Rosamund saw the beads of perspiration standing on the bony forehead. "What is it? What is it, my dear?" She looked toward the wood, then back to the child again. "There's nothing there."

Maggie came running down the path now, crying, "Wouldn't that curdle your blood? That's the third time she's done that this week. What is it, child?" Maggie was bending over her now. "What are you seeing? There's nothing there. Glory be to God, there's not a thing to be seen for miles except those few trees. What is it at all?"

The child was now clinging to Rosamund, her arms around her thighs, her head buried in her waist. "Something's frightened her," Rosamund said. "Perhaps it was an animal. Is she afraid of cattle?"

"Not a bit, not a bit. She would go and lie down with the cows themselves. But I'm tellin' you, this is the third time she's done it this week, and it's a different screaming."

"When she's been looking towards the wood?"

"No, no. She was sitting in the kitchen one evening having her supper, just about this time, before she was going up to bed. And she let out such a screech that, I'm tellin' you here and now, me heart nearly stopped dead in me."

"There, there, it's all over." Rosamund disengaged the child's arms from her, then led her up the drive and into the house. It took much longer tonight to get her off to sleep, and the nightjar was calling from the wood and the swallows flying low in the direction of the river when Rosamund came downstairs again. The sun had gone down, and already the hall was dim.

"You've had a time of it, then," Maggie greeted her when she entered the kitchen, "though you can handle her better than anyone I've seen, including himself. Which reminds me, it's black dark it's going to be afore he gets here and not a torch on him. God protect him, he'll end up in one of them ditches, the like of such I've never seen, and me that's lived in the bog country. I actually saw a man swallowed up in me youth, and yet the bog didn't put the fear of God in me like them ditches."

"I've no love for them either, Maggie. Although I like the fens, I wish they didn't have to have dykes. But, you know, that's what makes the fens, the dykes. But I shouldn't worry about Mr. Bradshaw."

"No, no. But, all the same, I wonder what's keeping him. Do you think he'll go into the village and see Mr. Gerald? For he said this morning it would be a gliff he would be gettin' when he heard the news. Do you like Mr. Gerald?"

Maggie looked at Rosamund with her head on one side.

"Yes, yes. He's very nice, very pleasant."

"Well, it may be news to you or not, but he thinks the same of you, and a bit more from the way he talks. He tells me he went swimming with you one night a while back."

"No, no." Rosamund turned quickly to the old woman. "No, he just happened to be passing when I was swimming and I sat talking to him for a while on the bank."

"Ah, well, I must have got it wrong, but he's been down there a number of times and I thought he was along with you."

"No, no, he wasn't with me, Maggie."

Rosamund had met Gerald Gibson a number of times

119

in the past few weeks and they had talked and laughed quite a bit, but for a reason she wouldn't allow herself to go into she had made sure that when she went swimming in the pond he wasn't there. At their second meeting she had gathered that Mr. Gerald, as Maggie called him, was a bit of a philanderer, that he wanted to flirt, without being taken seriously. She liked him up to a point and that was all.

Maggie began lighting the lamp and Rosamund said, "I don't suppose Mr. Bradshaw will be long now, and as Susie hasn't wakened up I think I'll be making my way home."

"Won't you wait and let him take you to the river? I wouldn't for the life of me cross that land in the dark."

"It isn't quite dark yet."

"Well, will you have one last look across the field for me and see if he's comin', for I won't feel at rest until he's here?"

"Yes, I'll do that." Rosamund smiled reassuringly at the old woman and went out into the hall.

She had just let the green baize door swing to behind her when her hand, flying to her throat, stifled a scream. Across the dimness of the hall, beyond the great bare window, stood a woman's figure, or—she closed her eyes for a second—*had* stood, for the figure was no longer there.

One hand still gripping her throat, the other hand tightly holding the front of her dress, and, righteous anger overcoming her shock, Rosamund made her way to the front door. Why couldn't Jennifer have rung the bell instead of sneaking about the place like that? She pulled open the door, and when she stepped outside and saw no one she stood for a moment slightly perplexed.

"Jennifer, Jennifer!" she called.

When there was no reply, she walked to the end of the house and in the direction of the back door. As she

120

reached it, Maggie called from the kitchen, "Is that you, Miss Rosie?"

"Yes, yes, it's me, Maggie. I—I was just walking round."

"Is he not to be seen then?"

"No, not yet. I'll go and have another look." She hurried now, almost at a run, to the front of the house again, then round to the buildings at the back, and here, keeping her voice down, she called again, "Jennifer! Jennifer!"

She had passed the front of the house once more and was half-way down the drive when she stopped. Looking towards the wood, she saw the scurrying, dim shape of Jennifer disappearing into it.

"Well! What on earth was she up to, sneaking around? What did she expect to see?" Rosamund muttered to herself, her anger was rising still further when it was checked by the thought: But she's afraid of the dark. She wouldn't come out on the fens at this time of night. . . . But she had. The face that had looked through the window was Jennifer's—she knew her sister. All this business of being afraid of the dark, afraid of the fens at night. Just wait till she saw her. . . .

She made her way quickly to the kitchen again, and, taking her coat from the back of the door, she said, "I'll be away now, Maggie. I'll see you in the morning."

"I wish you could stay until he comes. He'll have such news to tell."

"I'll hear it all tomorrow."

"Yes, you will, and let me say it's glad I am that you're comin' to look after the child."

"Thank you, Maggie. Good night."

"Good night, me dear. Good night and God look after ye across that wild land."

"You're stark staring mad. I tell you I've never been near the house."

121

"Don't lie to me, Jennifer. Look. Look at those shoes, they've got mud on them. You wouldn't get that unless you'd been down to the water."

"Well, I was down at the water, I was looking at the boat."

Rosamund's eyes narrowed as she looked at her sister, and she said slowly, "The boat was at the far side, remember? Naturally, when I went across I left it there. A few minutes ago it was on this side, I had to pull it over."

"All right! All right! I did use the boat. I did cross the river, if you want to know. But I didn't go to the house. I went——" Jennifer turned her head away. "I took the short-cut and went towards Andrew's."

Rosamund blinked for a moment before she asked quietly, "Did you see Andrew?"

"No, I didn't. I didn't go that far; I only got to the pond and then I turned back."

"And you came on to the house and had a look round."

"I didn't! I didn't!" Jennifer had swung round. "I tell you I never went near the house."

"I don't believe you. I saw you peering in at the window."

"You're mad. What would I want, peering in at the window?"

"That's what I'd like to know. You've been curious these past weeks because I've never mentioned anything about him, and it's set you wondering, hasn't it?"

The sitting-room door opened at this point and Henry Morley entered. "What's happening now?" he asked wearily.

"She's gone stark, staring mad, Father. She's accusing me of going over to the house and spying on her and that individual over there."

"I saw her looking through the window, Father."

"You did nothing of the sort, I've never been near the place."

122

"You were over the river, Jennifer," Henry stated, and Jennifer, lowering her head, said almost desperately, "Yes, yes. I was over the river; I've just told her why. I went as far as the pond and I came back. I—I intended going to Andrew's, but I didn't."

"Oh! Oh!" The second exclamation was a little louder. It said that Henry believed his daughter, and now he looked at Rosamund, adding: "You could have been mistaken, Rosie. Perhaps it was the old woman you saw."

"Oh, it doesn't matter, it doesn't matter." Rosamund turned from them abruptly and went up the stairs to her room.

She was too angry to go to bed. She did not relish being tossed and turned by the turmoil of her thinking. So she sat by the window, looking out across the dark land.

She had not been sitting long before she heard her father and Jennifer coming upstairs, and when their doors had closed on them she gave a deep sigh and some of the tension left her body.

She had been sitting at the window for over half an hour when the clock on the landing struck eleven. She shivered, and, reaching out, she pulled a rug from the foot of the bed, and wrapped it round her.

The moon had come out from behind the clouds, and as the far side of the river bank became visible to her, so did the figure standing on the landing stage. The sight of him brought her to her feet, but she remained still. The house was in shadow, and he would not be able to see her. Would he come across and knock them up? She had a sudden almost passionate longing for him to do just that. But the minutes passed and he made no move from the landing.

She turned her head and looked towards her bedroom door. If she tried to go out quietly they were bound to hear. But if she went downstairs ordinarily, as if she was going to the kitchen, they would take no notice. It wouldn't be the first time she had gone downstairs to make herself a drink when she couldn't sleep.

Keeping the rug around her, she went, not too quietly, out of the room and down the stairs. She went through the kitchen, unlocked the back door and moved cautiously round the side of the house, across the garden, and to the boat landing.

He was still standing on the far landing and he raised his hand to her. She gave him no return wave, but dropped quietly into the ferry. Slowly, evenly, hand over hand, she drew the boat across the water, making scarcely a ripple, and no sound at all from the heavy chain.

His hands were ready waiting for her when she reached the far bank, and when he pulled her up on to the landing she found she was trembling so much that she couldn't even whisper a greeting.

"I willed you to come out," he said very quietly.

"I can't stay long," Rosamund stammered. "I just wanted to know how you had got on."

"You're coming back to the house, I've got so much to tell you; but, more important still, I've brought some food back, real food: chicken, ham, wine. I didn't think you'd be gone. I got back as soon as I could."

"But it's so late."

"Late? It's just after eleven. And what does it matter, anyway?"

Yes, what did it matter? She turned and he took her arm as he had done earlier in the day, almost lifting her along the path. The excitement that was filling him found its way to her and she asked eagerly, "Was it very good news?"

"Ah, Rosie!" Her arm was pulled tightly against his side. "Very good news, indeed. I can't get used to it yet, but I soon will; oh yes, I soon will. I am a factory owner, Rosie. What do you think of that? And not just one factory. I have a tannery, a bag factory, a shoe factory, shares in chemicals and heaven knows what else, and at this moment reposing in a bank in Cambridge is an advance of twenty thousand pounds. Think of it, Rosie—twenty thousand pounds." She was pulled to a stop.

They had come to the edge of the wood now. His face was in shadow as he bent above her, and she could not see the expression in his eyes, but the tone of his voice caused her heart to race as he asked, "Who do you think I wanted with me in London today?"

She did not answer.

"When I came out of that solicitor's office and stood in the street like someone dazed, the first thought that came to my mind was: I can get away. The house could be furnished, the roof repaired, the land tilled, and it could all be done while I, Michael Bradshaw, was taking a long, long holiday abroad. I've always wanted money to enable me to travel. That is, until I came back to this God-forsaken, blood-sucking, heart-holding land. And then I thought . . . I wish Rosie was here. . . . Don't be afraid."

"I'm : . . I'm not afraid."

"Well, don't move away from me."

"I . . . I . . ."

"Look! Come on, let's eat and celebrate. Here, give me your hand!" He grabbed her hand and the next minute she was flying over the moonlit fields towards the broken gate and the drive. And, bubbling inside her there was laughter and excitement—and such happiness that she had never experienced before, did not know it was in her to experience. She was being almost choked by a feeling that was new, and even a little terrifying. She had said a moment earlier that she wasn't afraid. But she was afraid, she was afraid of him. Of his strength, his compellingness, his assertiveness that swept everything before it. But she was gasping and laughing out loud when he drew her to a halt at the front door. It was wide open, and the bare hall was streaked with moonlight. Still at a trot he led her across the hall and into the kitchen. The lamp was lit, and the table was set for a meal. He looked about him, saying, "Maggie must have gone up to bed already. She was tired, but she's tucked in, I see." He pointed to the roast chicken and the ham. Then, turning to Rosamund, he pulled her towards a chair, and, whipping the rug from her shoulders, said, "Sit yourself down there. We'll eat first and talk afterwards, eh?"

She watched him go to the sink and wash his hands before coming to the table. She watched him slice the ham and carve up the chicken. There were two bottles of wine on the table, and as he picked up one and held it to the light he cast his eyes on her and said, "Champagne is overrated, you can't better a good Auslese." His face was alight now with laughter, odd, satirical laughter, as he looked towards the delf rack and said, "Wine in teacups, thick ones at that—I never thought about the glasses. I imagined I had thought about everything, at least in the food line." As he poured the wine into the cups he went on, "You know, Rosie, I could have bought anything today—clothes for the child, a rig-out for Maggie, and furs"—he flicked his eyes down to her—"real ones, and diamonds to go with them, but what did I think of? Food. Good food. A square meal. It's a long, long time since I ate a proper meal. But now we can have chickens and steaks, until we're sick of the sight of them."

She watched him place the cups on the table, then, sweeping one arm towards her with a grandiose movement, he said, "Supper is ready. Allow me, madam."

One moment she was looking up at him with laughter quivering on her lips, the next she was struggling vainly to quell the choking feeling in her throat, for the lump that had suddenly lodged itself there threatened to stop her breathing. The torrent of tears washed over her with the force of a breaker, and her head was bowed under it almost to her knees as she tried to stifle her sobs with her hands across her mouth.

"Rosie! Rosie! God, don't cry like that! What is it? What have I done, what have I said? Rosie . . ." He was kneeling by her side. "What is it? Look at me. Tell me what it is."

Her face was now cupped in his hands, but she could see him only faintly through the blur of her tears. She could not tell him what had made her cry, she did not really know herself. The pathos in his attitude towards food perhaps. The elemental man in him who had put first things first. The boyishness so strong in the man. His strange tenderness. The derisiveness that touched everything he said. So many things had made her cry.

"Rosie . . ." He was drying her eyes and his voice was low. "Look at me, straight in the eyes."

Her body was still shaking with her emotions as she did as he asked.

"Will you marry me, Rosie?"

His eyes were deep and dark and held hers fast; there was no way of turning from them even if she had wanted to. She almost felt herself being drawn into their depths.

When she remained mute he said impatiently, "I'm not asking you to love me. We won't talk about love; that is something to be slopped over by the very young, and to be remembered by the old. We are in between the two and I'm past romance. But I have money now, enough to support a wife, as a wife should be supported." The derisiveness was back in his tone again, and as she gulped and shook her head he put in, "Oh, I know money doesn't mean all that to you, Rosie, but it's a great compensation. . . . There is the child."

"Don't. . . . Don't put it like that. I would have looked after the . . . the child if you hadn't a p-penny."

"Yes. Yes, I know that." His voice was deep and quiet as he spoke now, and without the slightest trace of mockery, "Yes, I know, because from the moment I saw you with her at the front door, your face full of compassion, I thought, Here is someone with a heart. And from that moment you had an effect upon me, you disturbed me greatly, filled me with restlessness whenever I couldn't see you, or know that you were near. I became as bad as the child for you. I wished at times I was like the child and you would take my hand and lead me. . . . Perhaps it is a mother I want."

"Michael, don't." She was in his arms, her head buried in his neck, repeating his name again and again, "Michael, Michael."

"You will marry me, then?"

"Oh yes; yes."

"You don't love me but you will marry me." Was there that cold laughter in his voice again?

"But I do . . . I do love you."

And she knew that she did. She knew that this was love. That this pain, this deep ache, this unsatisfied want, was love. She knew that this was what she had been waiting for, for days, perhaps weeks. When there was no other prospect but of living in this bare, empty-sounding house, she knew now that she had wanted to do just that so as to be near him. . . . What about Clifford? She could almost laugh aloud now at the thought of Clifford and her feeling for him. She would have to confess somewhat shamefacedly that security had been the main attraction where Clifford was concerned. Keeping the mill as a home for them all had been the star on that particular horizon. That, too, had been the cause of her recurring dream. But this, this feeling, this strange disturbing want —this was love.

He was holding her face once more in his hands. It was below his own now, and when quietly his lips touched hers she put her arms about his neck and with all her strength she held him to her.

When at last he released her she was overcome with a sudden shyness, and she would have turned from him to the table had he not pulled her round to face him again.

"We'll make it soon, Rosie. Special licence."

She nodded, unable to speak.

"It could be all fixed up in a week."

"A week?" Now her eyebrows went up just the slightest. "But they . . . I mean my father and Jennifer . . . they'll have to get used to the idea. I'm not quite sure whether they will like it at all; they've somehow got used to being looked after."

"Rosie." He pulled her down to the chair again, and, squatting on his heels before her and gripping her hands in his, he said urgently, "Don't tell them. Don't tell anyone. Let's do it on the quiet."

"But . . . but what'll they think?"

"Does it matter what they think, what anybody thinks? Rosie . . ." He released one hand and, putting it up to her face, stroked her cheek. "Do this for me, will you? You see, I've got a fear on me. Yes . . ." He closed his eyes for a moment and nodded his head. "As Maggie would say, I've a fear on me. It might appear that I'm afraid of nothing or no one, but I am. All my life I have found that anything I've wanted, and valued, has been taken from me, or spoiled in some way. . . ."

"But I won't . . . I won't, Michael. I'll . . ."

"I know, Rosie, I know." He patted her cheek as if she were the child. "I know I can trust you, but I can't trust fate. You see, this feeling goes a long way back with me, right to my childhood in this very house." He raised his eyes to the ceiling. "Some things stand out in my mind. The first was the boat. I always wanted a boat of my own. My father had enough money to buy me ten boats in those days. But no, he wouldn't hear of me having a boat, so, with the help of my mother, I saved up and bought one. I kept it at the end of the Cut. I kept it for one day at the end of the Cut. The second morning when I went to see it, it was a burnt-out shell. This kind of thing happened again and again. I wanted to go in for medicine, but all my father could think of was the land and the cheapest way to work it. I was just old enough to

129

get in at the tail-end of the war, and when I was de-mobbed and came back here I knew I couldn't stick it. Then my mother died and left me the little that she had, and I made the break and started my studies in London. There was nothing I wanted more in life than to become a doctor, and not just a doctor, a surgeon. . . . In my second year up there I met Susie's mother." He turned his eyes away from Rosamund at this point, and his voice went deeper into his throat as he said, "I look back now and say to myself, 'You of all people should have been able to resist fascination. You of all people should have been able to discern what lay behind beautiful shells.' But apparently I couldn't, for I went down like corn under the blade." He looked at Rosamund again. "I'm making no excuses for myself. Everything was forgotten, I went mad. She had a little money, and with what I had left it was enough to keep us on the move abroad for a time, but long before the child was born the money was finished, and so was I. I had woken up as if from a drugged dream. Yet life was bearable in some ways, until Susan came. . . . From the minute that child drew breath her mother hated her. It became so intense that it turned her brain before she died. . . ." He paused and drew in a long breath before adding, "She was drowned. . . ."

After a silence that seemed to Rosamund impossible to penetrate, he went on, "It was strange, but the more she hated the child the more I loved her—the child I mean, not the mother. In the end I hated Camilla with a hatred that equalled her own for the child. It was odd, but I'd always craved for children, and I remember thinking that I would put up with Camilla if she gave me a family . . particularly daughters." He smiled sadly. "I had a fancy for daughters. The psychological answer there is that I loved my mother and hated my father. Well, I got a daughter as you know, Rosie." He was looking at her again. "Do you see what I mean about fate? I wish . . . I get my wish, but fate gives it a twist." He was gripping

130

her hands once more. "It mustn't happen again, Rosie, you understand? . . . It mustn't happen again. Your father will put up all kinds of objections, he will point out Susie to you. . . ."

"No, no, he won't; he understands. . . ."

He was shaking his head vigorously now. "Then there's your sister, she has no love for me. My manner with her was very cursory at our first meeting—you will know all about that, I suppose. She'll put her spoke in. . . ."

She too was shaking her head as she checked his rapid flow, saying, "Listen, listen, Michael. Nobody will stop me doing what I want. I want . . . I want to marry you, Michael, but . . . All right, all right." The last words were wrenched from her by the look in the depths of his eyes, and it was she now who put out her hand and touched his cheek. "It will be as you say—I'll tell no one."

He brought her hand around to his mouth and pressed his lips to the palm. A second later, pulling her to her feet again, he cried jovially, "Let's drink to us." But when with the cup in his hand he clinked hers, he said softly and with deep feeling, "No, not to us; to Rosie . . . Mrs. Michael Bradshaw."

She was in her room once more, undressing as if she was still in a dream, the dream of the past two hours, when her bedroom door was thrust open and Jennifer, a candle in her hand, her face tight and almost vicious in its expression, came into the room. Rosamund looked at her sister for some time, waiting for her to speak, and when she did her words were like drops of acid.

"No wonder you were afraid of being spied upon; your guilty conscience had every right to make you furious."

"All right! All right! You know where I've been, so what about it?" Although Rosamund's head was up and her chin high, her voice was quiet, but not so Jennifer's as she went on:

"Sneaking out of the house, and creeping across the

131

river without a sound and him waiting for you. You needn't deny it."

"Who's denying it?"

"You're mad. He can't afford to furnish the house let alone employ anyone. Three pounds a week. . . . Huh! What is he expecting for his three pounds, I wonder?"

The cry that escaped Rosamund checked Jennifer's vitriolic words, and she turned her head away from the onslaught of Rosamund's tongue. Rosamund's anger and indignation was so great that she hardly knew what she was saying herself, but as her father appeared behind Jennifer in the doorway she was crying, "What you're afraid of is being left here to see to Father, and that's what'll happen to you, just that."

"What is it? What on earth is it? What is the matter with you, anyway?" Henry Morley pushed past Jennifer and stood between them.

"I've been out, Father; I've just come back. I've been having supper with Mr. Bradshaw, Michael Bradshaw. Jennifer saw me go out and she likely saw me come back."

"Yes . . . yes, I did. . . . Kissing on the bank, and you haven't known him five minutes . . . and supposed to hate his guts."

"I never said I hated his guts, not once, never. . . . And, yes, we were kissing on the bank. Is there anything wrong in that?" She was looking at her father now, and, apparently, if not finding it wrong, Henry Morley was finding it rather mystifying, for his voice was puzzled as he asked, "You and him . . . Bradshaw? Oh, Rosie! And . . . and there's the child."

"I know there's the child. I've always known there's the child, Father."

"All right! All right, Rosie, don't shout at me. I'm not saying anything against the child. I pity it. But him . . . Bradshaw. . . . What about Clifford?"

"Yes, what about Clifford, Father? I can tell you now

132

that the only thing I wanted Clifford for was to secure this house for us all. But with Michael it's different. It was different from the beginning. I knew he had nothing. I knew he'd be no means of security. Perhaps for me because I wanted very little . . . but not with both of you added on." She wagged her hand between them. "It's yourselves you've thought of all along, what's going to happen to you. I was just the one who solved the problems. I've felt old before my time solving your problems. I was the go-between with Uncle Edward—Uncle Edward, who could make things happen because he had money. I liked Uncle Edward for himself, but I hated being dependent on him. . . ." She just stopped herself in time from finishing, "I could earn a living anywhere."

"Your past problems will be nothing to your future ones." Jennifer was about to turn away on this last cutting remark when she was stopped by Rosamund saying very quietly, "There you are mistaken. Why he wanted to see me tonight . . . why he came to the ferry, was to tell me the result of his visit to London. He's no longer without money. He's rich. Do you hear? Rich. He can do anything he wants." She looked directly at Jennifer now as she said, "He can travel." And immediately she reproached herself for her cattiness, for Jennifer's face tightened even more. She was about to make some retort when her Father said, "Are you serious about this man, Rosie?"

Rosie wanted to cry at them both, "Yes, yes, I am serious. We're going to be married," but the promise she had made checked her, and for answer she said, "He has offered me a good post."

"Huh!"

Her Father and Jennifer, both with their backs to her, were on the landing now and the "huh!" coming from Jennifer angered Rosamund so much that she cried at them, "And tomorrow morning when you get up I'll be gone."

"What!"

They had both swung round, the same expression threaded across their faces, and the apprehension that Rosamund saw there made her want to run to them, take their hands and cry, "Listen, listen to my wonderful news, we're all going to be all right." But the time was not now, so, dropping her head, she modified her threat by adding, "I'm going into Cambridge to help . . . help choose some furniture." Her eyes too were cast down as she made this admission, but when neither of them spoke she added sharply and with a touch of bitterness, "But don't worry, it'll be all right and proper, we're taking the child with us. That should set your fears at rest."

When in the dim flickering candlelight she saw them go their separate ways across the landing, she went quickly to her door and closed it, and, standing with her back to it, her hands joined tightly together, she whispered aloud, "Oh why, oh why, does it have to be like this? They're spoiling it for me." It was just as Michael had said, if they knew she was going to be married they'd put all kinds of obstacles in her way. Or would they, now that they knew he was rich? Oh! Why was she thinking like this? It made her feel horrible.

Pulling herself from the door and undressing quickly, she got into bed, and in a few minutes her mind had left them—she made it leave them. Or were her thoughts actually lifted from her and taken over the fenlands to the bare house? He had said, "I willed you to come out", and now it was as if her father and Jennifer did not exist. She was with him again in the kitchen, hearing him say, "Will you marry me, Rosie?" He had not said, "I love you, Rosie." He had been honest and admitted he was past silly romance. But he would love her, she would make him. Even now he must love her a little, but, being of the nature he was, would not admit it. How else could he have asked her to be his wife?

She was dropping off to sleep when, the control of her

thoughts slackening, the answer was flung at her as she heard his voice saying as it had done only a short while ago, "Perhaps it's a mother I want."

In marrying her he would not only be getting a nurse for Susan, but a mother for the little boy in him. The selfish, egotistical, demanding little boy.

8

Rosamund seemed to be swimming in a sea of uncertain happiness. When at times she was overcome by fear, as if suddenly finding herself out of her depth, she would re-assure herself and say, "Just go steadily on, it'll all come right." She had the conviction that, once married to Michael, everything would settle into place, and she longed for the next few days to pass. Her marriage, when dwelt upon, would cause her to shiver with a mixture of delight, apprehension, and longing. But generally there was little time now to sit down and think quietly, for Michael, in a spate of spending, was transforming Thornby House. In the midst of all the bustle she would sometimes stop and try to remember what the house was like a week ago. The desolation, the emptiness, the coldness of it. Now all that was changed. Knocking and hammering seemed to come from its every corner. There seemed to be painters and paper-hangers everywhere inside the house. And outside there were now four men working on the land, and only yesterday a new machine had arrived. Moreover, there was a car turning up its long snooty nose at being housed in the old barn. Overall there was a feeling of excitement pervading the atmosphere, and rather oddly an air of happiness too. The men whistled at their work. Maggie shouted and chaffed with everyone within radius. Everybody seemed happy and natural, everyone except Michael, and herself at times, when she realized she was playing a part, the essential of which was the deception of her father and Jennifer.

Michael never touched her, not even her hand, in front of others. Not until last thing at night when he was taking her back to the river in the dark did he come closer than an arm's length of her. It was strange, she thought at times, that his manner was more stiff now than it had been before he asked her to marry him. She had hinted that she would like him to come across the river and see her father, as if on an ordinary visit, but he had not taken to this suggestion either. When they were married, yes, but not before, not before.

The men, making a concerted effort in the house, had yesterday finished one room, and when at noon today some of the furniture had arrived he had asked her to see to the arranging of it. He had spoken as if she had not seen the stuff before, as if every single piece but one had not been her choice. The workmen had been present, and he had addressed her as Miss Morley, saying, "Miss Morley will show you where it has to go." Miss Morley knows this, Miss Morley knows that. The only thing he himself had directed was the moving of the small baby grand. When, the piano assembled, he had run a practised hand over the keys, it had come to her that there were lots of things about this man she did not know. Evidently he played and liked playing the piano.

It was long past five o'clock, but the men were still working, and as Rosie listened to the hammering and their distant voices she thought, and somewhat sadly at this point, that it was amazing what money could do. This time last week there hadn't been enough food in the house, and now men were working overtime. In a few minutes a lorry would come, and they would all pile into it and be taken to the main road. The money had even made a rough road across two fields to allow passage for the vehicles. Not only that, it had spanned the dyke with great planks of wood, a temporary affair while the bridge was being repaired. Money was like magic, like oil, it made the wheels turn, oh, so easily. She mustn't be cynical about money, she told herself, but give it the respect due to it, that and no more.

The child came running with its unwieldy gait across the hall, crying, "Bov. Bov." This strange syllable was Susie's name now for Rosamund. All the child's utterances were staccato and short sounding, but "Bov" was distinctly meant for Rosamund, and she always answered to it.

"Oh, what have you got there? Oh, aren't they lovely!" She bent down and took the extended flowers from the child's hand. They were a mixture of rag-wort, dandelion, purple grass and wild foxgloves.

"Bov."

"Yes, dear, thank you very much. We must put them in water. Come along."

Today the child seemed happy and contented, but last night she'd had another of her screaming fits—one so intense that it had completely exhausted her. It had taken place when she was once again in sight of the wood. It was as if she was always seeing something in the wood. Yet she had these bouts at other times too. The evening they were returning from Cambridge she had been walking between them, a hand in each of theirs, when she had pulled herself to a stop, became rigid for a moment while she appeared to sniff the air, then let out a most blood-curdling scream. Although at the time they were within their own boundary they were not within sight of the house, or the wood.

When Rosamund had seen Jennifer looking through the window that evening she had, for a time, blamed her for the child's hysterics. It was evident that Susie had taken a dislike to Jennifer and the sight of her could evoke the scream. But Rosamund had now to discard this explanation. The child screamed when there was no one to be seen, no stranger. Yet how could they say that there was no one to be seen. She definitely was seeing someone or something. It was as if she smelt a presence. This eerie thought made Rosamund shudder, and yet the child did not have that effect on her. Even when she had first looked at the distorted face she had not shuddered. And now she saw the child as part of Michael and her compassion was threaded with love. But she shuddered at whatever it was that caused Susie to emit that terrible scream.

They had almost reached the kitchen when a voice from the doorway brought them round.

"Well, well, well, what d'you know?"

She laughed as she greeted Gerald Gibson, and cried childishly to him, "Surprise! Surprise!"

As he came up to her he cocked his head on one side, and, looking at her through narrowed lids, he repeated, "Surprise? Surprise indeed. I can't get over it. Mike's just been telling me. I didn't know what had hit the place when I saw all the bustle, and at this time of night. And you . . . have you come into a fortune too? You look positively glamorous!"

"What, in this?" She lifted one end of her overall up, then, shaking her head at him, she added, "It would take a lot of money to make me look glamorous."

"Well, if it isn't glamour you certainly have acquired something."

She turned her face quickly from him as she said, "It's the excitement. And who wouldn't be excited? It's like a fairy-tale. Have you had any tea?"

"Yes. Yes, thanks. I had it before I left home."

Maggie greeted the visitor with, "There you are then, Mr. Gerald, and what do you think of the news, eh? Who would believe that such things happen? But God's good, and He sees to His own, He does. Sometimes, mind, He takes His time over it." She laughed and pushed at Gerald's shoulder vigorously, almost overbalancing him.

"Maggie"—he now teased her—"I think it's the worst possible thing that could have happened. You'll now eat so much you won't be able to move that carcass of yours."

"Aw, away with you. I'll move me carcass, never you fear. Now I must go and find himself and see if he's not ready for something to eat."

When Maggie had left the kitchen, Gerald, looking across at Rosamund, remarked caustically, "My! My! My! Aren't we all merry and bright! Not a cloud in the sky."

Rosamund, turning her head quickly towards him, realized that Mr. Gerald wasn't too pleased at his friend's changed circumstances.

He might have read her scrutiny, for he changed the conversation from Michael to herself by saying, "Have you got that cousin of yours staying with you?"

"My cousin? No, what makes you ask that?"

"Oh, you once remarked that your cousin used to berth his boat at the bottom of the Cut, and there's one there now. It's a Banham's hired craft. Though this one's not exactly at the bottom of the Cut, but just a little way along the bank, up near the staunch. What made me think that it might be your cousin's is that I saw your sister leaving it. I was some way off and I tried to catch her up, but she was too quick for me. I've never really met her, only seen her from across the river. She's quite a good-looking miss, isn't she? You know, you've never asked me across to meet her."

No, thought Rosamund, and I'm not going to. There was enough trouble between Jennifer and Andrew without Gerald Gibson complicating matters still further. So she evaded the latter part of the question and replied, "Yes, yes, she is very good-looking."

Gerald Gibson's news about the boat was rather startling. Clifford must have come. What was she going to say to him? What could she say to him? . . . "You are three weeks too late." No, she wouldn't go into it. She would just say no. That's if he asked her before Monday. On Monday, when she came back from Cambridge, she would say to him, "I am married." The thought sent a spiralling wave of heat through her. It had the power to flush her face and bring forth comment from Gerald.

"Ah! Ah! Have I stumbled on the reason for all this gaiety? Not my friend Mike's money, but the cousin, in the cutter, at the bottom of the Cut." His high laugh at his own joke was checked by Rosamund's voice remarking with chilling flatness. "Whatever the reason for my jollity I can assure you it has nothing to do with my cousin."

"Oh?" He raised his eyebrows and remained silent for a moment, then added, "Can't blame a fellow for guessing, can you?"

Rosamund turned away. Funny, but she didn't like Gerald Gibson—at least at this moment she didn't like him. She had up to now thought he was good fun, but now she wondered. She wondered, too, about the sincerity of his friendship with Michael when he said, "What's all the to-do about in the house? Why all the rush, anyway? It's not likely that he'll stay here if he has enough money to get away. He's a strange bird, is Mike, flying too fast and too far for anyone to keep a tab on him."

"I don't see how he can fly very fast or very far with . . ." She cast her eyes to where the child was sitting in the corner of the chair playing with her doll. "And, anyway, I thought you had his welfare at heart, and that you'd be glad of his changed luck."

"I have, of course I have, and I am glad. What makes you think I'm not? What's the matter with you? Why are you on the defensive all of a sudden?"

Before she had time to answer the door opened and Maggie came in, saying, "He's as hungry as ten buffaloes, he says. Let me get the table set. It's steak he wants, with onions and mushrooms. Oh my, doesn't it make your mouth water . . .?"

The evening that followed was not what could be termed a success. Michael, she felt, overdid the Miss Morley, and she knew that his attitude was puzzling Gerald Gibson, for he had been much more free and easy with her when poverty was his lot. Now it must appear that the money had gone slightly to his head. Yet she knew that Gerald Gibson would know more of this man than she did, and would not be satisfied that this was so.

Long before it was dark she spoke of her intention of going home. She did this because she did not want the position to arise where Gerald Gibson would surely offer to see her to the river bank, with or without Michael being there. So, making the excuse that she would like to get home early, as she thought her cousin had arrived, she prepared to go.

She had run upstairs to have one last look at the child and was quietly crossing the landing towards the stairs again, when the sound of the piano being played came to her. She stopped still at the head of the stairs listening. It was beautiful, beautiful. She did not know what it was he was playing, but it had a soothing, lulling sound. She moved quietly now down the stairs and towards the open door of the sitting-room. Michael was at the piano, his profile to her. His powerful thick fingers were moving somewhat stiffly over the keys, yet bringing from them music which she knew to be good. Gerald Gibson was lolling back in an armchair smoking a cigarette, a glass of whisky to the side of him, and his eyes were on her as she looked towards Michael. But Michael did not look at her, he continued to play.

For a moment she forgot that there was anyone but themselves in the room and, moving to his side, she asked softly, "What is that?" He did not stop playing, nor look at her as he replied, "*Berceuse*. Tchaikovsky's *Berceuse*."

141

His voice was dreamy as he ended, ". . . it's my favourite. It was the first piece I ever heard played at a concert and it put me to sleep. My name for it since then has been 'Sleep Music'."

"Sleep Music. . . . Yes, it's like that, it's lovely."

She remained still for a time conscious only of the melody and of his hands lifting and falling, until once again she became aware of Gerald watching her, then she said, "I'll be going. Good night."

When Michael did not answer she turned away, filled now with pain. All her body seemed to be aching. She had a lost, lonely, unwanted feeling, and she hated Gerald Gibson.

"Rosie."

The music had stopped abruptly, and she turned at the doorway and looked at him. He was still sitting at the piano but half-swivelled round towards her. His eyes were dark and bright, and he said now, "Good night, Rosie."

The pain vanished, she swallowed, smiled, and said, "Good night." Then, turning her head briefly in Gerald Gibson's direction, she added, "Good night," and left the house. . . .

When she reached the river bank and saw Andrew sitting on the lawn talking to her father, she knew an immeasurable feeling of relief. When the ferry reached the other side Andrew was there to give her a hand up.

"Nice seeing you, Andrew."

"You too, Rosie."

"It's been a lovely day."

"Yes, but I think we've had all we're going to get. This can't go on for ever, you know."

She laughed merrily. "There speaks the farmer. . . . Hello, Father."

"Hello, Rosie. Had a nice day?" His voice was ordinary.

"Yes, a very nice day." Her answer implied nothing

other than it had been a day of familiar rounds. "Where's Jennifer?"

"That's what we're wondering."

"Wondering?" She looked from one to the other, then, turning her eyes from her father, she asked, "Has Clifford not arrived then?"

"Clifford?" Her father screwed his face up at her. "What makes you ask a question like that?"

She was looking back at him as she said, "Oh well, Mr. Gibson, a visitor, said that he saw a motor cruiser at the bottom of the Cut, a Banham's, and he thought he saw Jennifer on it. That's where Clifford always berths, and I thought . . . well . . ."

"I passed the bottom of the Cut and I didn't see any cruiser. When was this?"

"I don't know, Andrew, and I don't think it's exactly at the bottom of the Cut—a little way along towards the staunch."

"Oh, then I could have missed it. It would be round the bend."

"What time did he see her down there?" Her father was speaking again.

"Oh, I should have said around tea-time, judging by the time Mr. Gibson arrived at the house."

"It wasn't Jennifer." Henry Morley shook his head vigorously. "She never left the workroom until about an hour ago, and she hadn't left the house until just on fifteen minutes before Andrew came. She must have gone one way and Andrew come the other, or else they would have met. Whoever the fellow saw getting on that boat wasn't Jennifer."

Well, that was that. There was someone berthed at the bottom of the Cut and it wasn't Clifford, and for this she felt understandable relief. But what began to niggle at her mind was the fact that someone else besides herself had imagined they had seen Jennifer in a place where she couldn't possibly have been. . . .

143

When an hour later Jennifer had still not returned, Andrew, about to take his departure, said quietly, "Do you think she's purposely avoiding me, Rosie?"

"No, no, Andrew, get that out of your head. She's definitely been waiting for you coming, and she's been worrying. Oh, she's been worrying, Andrew, I can tell you that. She's likely gone the river way, and you, braving The Tiger"—she laughed at this—"cut across by the pond."

"Well, I thought I would have more chance of coming up with her that way."

"How is our friend Janice?" She looked at him with an amused twist to her lips.

"Oh . . . Janice. Janice is still going strong."

"Still on the chase?"

"Well, I wouldn't exactly say that, but she visits us at times. She's very interested in cattle, you know." He nodded his head as he returned her twinkle.

"I bet she is."

"Oh, Rosie, now don't be feminine." He gave her a gentle punch with his fist, then, stepping back and surveying her, he said, "You're liking this job across there, aren't you?" He motioned with his head across the river.

Her lids dropped for a second as she replied, "Yes. Yes, Andrew, I'm liking it very much."

"I knew you were. You look different. When I saw you coming across earlier I said to myself, Something's happened, Rosie looks . . . well . . . different. I don't mean that you have changed fundamentally . . ." He laughed. "You'll always be the same, Rosie. But—well—mind, I'm not just saying this—for a moment you looked every bit as beautiful as Jennifer."

Her head was back, and her laugh was ringing high; she was both pleased and amused as she said, "You qualified it, Andrew. 'For a moment' you said, and that's true."

"Come now, you know what I meant, Rosie. And it's the truth, I do mean it. Well, anyway, if you looked like a

144

sack of rotten beet you'd still have your personality left, Rosie, and that's everything."

Her laughter went higher and higher. "A sack of rotten beet. Oh, Andrew, you are funny."

"I suppose I am." His voice was quiet and he nodded to himself. "I'm not a bloke for paying compliments—that's why Jennifer got so fed up, I suppose. I could tell her with my eyes that she was beautiful, but I couldn't get it out of my mouth."

"You're going to change all that, aren't you?"

"I'm going to have a damned good try. . . . But just the once more, mind, like I said."

"Go on then, and go by the river. If she went that way she'll come back that way. Good night, Andrew."

"Good night, Rosie. . . . Good night there, Henry."

Henry Morley, straightening his back, waved the hoe as he cried, "Good night, Andrew. See you soon, I hope."

"Yes, I'll see you soon."

Andrew was gone, and as she went into the house she prayed that he and Jennifer would meet. Get that settled and there would be a load off her mind. There would only be her father then. Well, she had plans for him, and she felt she knew Michael well enough to be sure that he would fall in with her plans.

It was almost dark when Jennifer returned, and Rosamund saw immediately that she was in a very poor frame of mind.

"Did you meet Andrew?"

Jennifer jerked her head round and, staring blankly at her, said, "No, I didn't meet Andrew."

"Well, he's been here for the last hour and a half."

"I hope he enjoyed himself."

"Oh, don't be so childish, Jennifer. He came to see you. You must have gone one way and he came the other."

Jennifer stood for a moment looking down, then, dropping into a chair, she buried her face in her hands and began to sob brokenly.

"Oh, don't! Don't, Jennifer!" Rosamund had an arm around her. "Look, everything's going to be all right; he's as miserable as you are. And I'm going to tell you something. Look at me." She raised her sister's face upwards, and, although she knew she was giving Andrew away, she felt that there was a great need at this moment to do something to lift Jennifer's moral and self-esteem. "Now listen. You remember that night I came back and I said I'd met Andrew and Janice Hooper down by the bridge?" Jennifer made no answer, but lowered her wet lids, and Rosamund went on, "Well, he asked me that night to tell you that he was with Janice. He was getting a bit tired of your dillying and dallying, Jennifer, and he wanted to pull you up."

"But he was . . . he was with her, wasn't he?"

"Yes, he was, but it was just circumstantial, and I think it was very clever of old Andrew to make something out of it. You know, Andrew isn't just the quiet easy-going individual you take him for. He loves you deeply, but you mustn't play about with him any more, Jennifer, it would be too risky. Now listen. . . . Tomorrow morning you're going to go across there . . . you're going to walk right to that farm and see him."

Jennifer did not protest against this arrangement. There was no proud retort that she wasn't going to do any such thing. She merely dried her eyes calmly, and, saying quietly, "I think I'll go to bed," she went upstairs.

Well, that was that. At last Jennifer was seeing reason. Everything would be all right in that quarter . . . she hoped.

Rosamund now went into the sitting-room to say good night to her father, and impulsively she threw her arms around his neck and kissed him. And as he held her tightly to him, he looked at her and asked, "Are you happy, Rosie?"

Her gaze was averted from him, but she nodded her head rapidly, saying, "Very, very happy, Father."

146

"Thank God for that. If anybody's deserved it you have."

He had not asked what was making her happy, and she hadn't told him. Her father was really no fool. She went upstairs, her heart singing.

9

Andrew's prophesy came true, and Jennifer's decision to go and visit him the following morning was prevented.

Rain never comes at the right time for farmers. They want rain in one field and sunshine in another. Winter or summer, rain in moderation is nearly always welcomed by them, but when it passes this point it becomes a danger, and more so to the men who till the fenlands.

For three days and three nights it had rained, with hardly a let-up. The tidal part of the river above Erith was suffering badly; already many fields in that quarter were under water. The main River Ouse, going towards Denver Sluice, was just holding its own. But the Little Ouse River, which is the continuation of Brandon Creek, the latter a tributary of the main Ouse, had swollen in some places to three times its width. Also part of the newly made bank of the Old West River beyond Dale's Inn had been swept away, and the men were having a job to stem the flow. It was when the water flooded in from the cuts and dykes into the already swollen river that the situation became dangerous. For often the main sluice at Denver had to contend with tides that were higher than the level of the river water. Then the danger hours were when the swollen water from the river could not be released.

Even the water in the Cut had risen, and now covered the landing-stages on each bank and was moving threateningly across the garden. The old mill wheel had once coped with such a situation as this, but how effectively Rosamund, looking at the rising water, was given to doubt. For the diesel-driven machines installed in most of the wheel-houses dotting the fens now, were hard put to it to cope. The sluices were being watched night and day, and the men working on the house had said yesterday that it could be the beginning of another nineteen forty-seven. The only thing to be thankful for was it was summer, and not spring, as in that fateful year of fenland flooding and havoc. . . . And it was her wedding day.

As Rosamund looked out of the window over the sodden water-soaked land, she thought, This is my day and it looks as if the whole world is weeping.

When she went downstairs she was wearing her ordinary clothes; her new clothes were over at the house waiting for her. Her father and Jennifer were just finishing breakfast, and Henry Morley turned to her and said, "Isn't it risky going across there when it's like this?"

"It isn't any worse than yesterday."

"It will be over your wellingtons before you get to the boat."

"No, I don't think so."

Even if the water was pouring into her wellingtons she would still cross the river this morning. She would cross the river if she had to swim.

When she was ready she turned and looked at them, and the desire to tell them was almost overwhelming. She wanted to say, "Wish me happiness." This was her wedding day, they should be with her. She felt a moment of acute guilt, and her conscience cried, It isn't a good thing you're doing, keeping them in the dark like this. Yet what could she do? She had promised Michael faithfully that she would tell no one, not until they came back. She

148

said now, "I'll be going into Cambridge today. Is there anything you want?"

Both of them appeared to stop and think, and then one after the other they told her there was nothing they could think of.

"All right. Goodbye."

"Goodbye."

"Goodbye."

There was nothing they could think of, but she could think of things they wanted. When Michael came over with her later today, she would bring across a drop of whisky, and all of the tobacco her father could smoke for a month. Michael had said to her only last night when she had told him a little of her father's struggle against his weakness, "It's a bad thing, you know, to deprive a man of it altogether. A little now and again would do him no harm, and save him a great deal of torment, I'm sure." Michael was right.

And Jennifer. What would she bring Jennifer? All Jennifer seemingly wanted now was Andrew, and by hook or by crook she'd get Andrew here tonight if they had to paddle all the way up the Cut, for she knew that she couldn't enjoy her happiness unless both Jennifer and her father were happy too.

The boat was not now attached to the chain but to a rope; and when it ground to a stop on the mud of the bank she scrambled over the side, and, paying out the rope, took it to a stake they had placed some distance away. She was in the process of tying the rope securely to the stake when the action recalled something to her mind. It had been as she was untying the rope last night that she had raised her head and seen Gerald Gibson hurrying towards her from out of the wood—not from the direction of the house, but from the path that led to the pond. He had run the last few yards to her, and when he reached her side she noticed that he was rather pale and was not his cheery facetious self. She had asked

149

immediately, "Is anything the matter?" and he had rubbed his hand across his mouth before saying, "I've just had a bit of a shock." And then he had asked an odd question, "Is your sister in?" She had told him that she didn't know as she was just going across to the house, but with the water rising as it was she was nearly sure to be indoors. He had then asked if she would make sure. His words brought to her a feeling of fear that she could not analyse at the moment, and checked her from questioning him further. After crossing the river and finding Jennifer in the kitchen, she had come on to the front steps again and signalled to him that she was at home. She had said nothing to Jennifer about this, but it had troubled her for some time until it had become overshadowed in the anticipation of today. Now the memory was vividly back with her. She did not know when she had actually stopped liking Gerald Gibson, but she was certainly aware that she no longer was amused by him, or thought him a pleasant companion. Was it because of his implied criticism of Michael? Yes, perhaps. One thing she was sure of: Gerald Gibson was certainly not over-pleased at his friend's good fortune. She felt that he was more than a little jealous of Michael. But the question was, why had he asked if Jennifer was in the house?

Her mind was relieved of its uneasy probing by the sight of Michael coming towards her from the far side of the wood. She wanted to hold out her arms and run to him, but his manner always quelled spontaneity in her, and more so this morning. So she walked, even sedately, towards him.

"You're soaked already." He was looking her up and down.

"I can't see that you're much better yourself." She smiled at him, then screwed up her face as she took in his mud-spattered breeches and coat. "You've been working?"

"Since five."

"Where? What's happened?"

"I got the idea that if the dyke in the end field was cleared it would heighten the banks there, and at the same time it might relieve just a little water from the Goose Pond. I made a start on it and got all the men going as they arrived."

"From the house, the painters?"

"The lot. They all came in rubber-boots knowing what the road was like. Things are looking rather black in some quarters, I'm afraid. Some of the cottagers have already moved to the villages."

She stared up at him a moment before saying, "What about . . . will it make any . . .?"

Her words were cut off as he laughed and ended for her, "Make any difference? Do you want it to? Come on, tell me, do you?"

"No. No, of course I don't, Michael."

"Very well then, we'll be at that church, Rosie, at eleven o'clock even if we have to take a boat down the river."

She felt self-conscious and a little ashamed at her apparent eagerness, but he did not appear to notice, and his dark eyes smiled at her as he went on, "And it looks pretty much like that even now, for we can't use the car. The road isn't too bad, but I'm afraid of the old bridge. Half the bank on the far side is gone, and I doubt if it'll hold any weight. The men left the lorry on yon side this morning . . . wisely too. . . . Anyway, no matter how we get to Ely, we get there, and by eleven o'clock." With an unexpected, swift movement he pulled her close to him, and, looking down on her face, he said with mock seriousness, "And I'm thinking of no one but that minister. He's gone to a lot of work to hurry up this business. Special licences in churches these days take a little time. And I don't think at first the bishop was satisfied with my need for urgency, but the threat of the registry office did it." He nodded at her, and for a second she leant her brow against his neck. She had expressed the wish that

151

she would like to be married in a church, and he must have gone to quite a deal of trouble, and put others to the same, to grant this wish.

"You frightened, Rosie?"

"Frightened?" She brought her face up quickly to his. "Frightened? No." She was not speaking the truth and to give stress to her statement she added another "No".

Gently he wiped the rain from her cheeks. "You wouldn't like to back out? There's still time, and there's the child."

"Oh, Michael, don't keep reminding me of the child, please. She's there and I love her. Yes, I really love her. You mightn't believe that, but I do."

"I believe you, Rosie. The only thing is you seem . . . well, too good to be true. You love the child, and you like me. . . . It seems too much to believe in all at once . . . yet I believe you."

Abruptly now, he turned away, grabbing hold of her arm as he did so. This was a peculiar trait in him, Rosamund found. When he touched her, he always held on to her as if she were trying to escape. At times he hurt her, and when he became aware of this he would drop his hold as if she had burnt him. He said briskly now, "I'd better put in an appearance at the dyke again before I change, but you get ready." And then he checked their steps for a moment adding, and rather sadly, she thought, "It'll be straight back for us. Do you mind?"

"No. No. It doesn't matter, not in the least." She smiled up at him reassuringly. And it didn't matter . . . not in the least. The only thing that mattered was that she should marry him at eleven o'clock that morning.

Rosamund felt slightly faint as she listened to the words: "I pronounce you man and wife." And things weren't very clear to her after this until she stood in the vestry signing the register. It was the laughter that brought her to the present, Michael's deep hard laugh.

The little minister's chuckle. The hicky-laugh of the cleaning woman, and the definite ha-ha-ha of the verger. It was over something the minister had said, but she couldn't remember what it was.

"Goodbye, Mrs. Bradshaw, I hope we'll see you in the church again soon."

"Yes." Her voice seemed rather hoarse. "Yes, I'll come again . . . we'll come again."

"And I hope I'll see you at Thornby House." Michael was shaking the minister's hand. "Don't forget you promised to pay us a visit."

"I won't forget, definitely not."

And when they stood outside the church, and the verger, pointing up at the sky, cried, "Look, it's stopped raining, and I believe, I do believe, that the sun will be out in a minute or so—isn't that a good omen?" Rosamund could have reached up and kissed the tall gangling man. When after thanking the woman once more she said goodbye to her, she judged from the warmth of her farewell that Michael's generosity had been lavish, and not to the woman alone.

They walked some distance along the street past the cathedral and into an hotel without exchanging a word. Lunch had been ordered, and not until they were seated at the table did he speak directly to her.

"How does it feel?"

"Wonderful."

"Don't tell fibs, you don't feel any different." His voice was a jocular whisper now.

"I do." She joined in with his mood, it helped to allay the fluttering uneven beating of her heart. "I'm amazed at myself, I've married the Fen Tiger. . . ." She bit on her lip as soon as she had said it. Then, dropping her head, she put her closed fist to her mouth to suppress her laughter.

"The . . . What did you say?" He was leaning towards her.

She was still laughing and kept her eyes from him as she said, "You heard."

"You thought of me as a fen tiger?"

"*The* Fen Tiger . . . there's a distinction."

He reached out and took her hand now. "What do you know about fen tigers?"

"Oh, quite a lot. I have listened to this one, and that one, and I've read quite a bit."

"So you think I'm a fen tiger . . . *The* Fen Tiger . . . the father of them all, eh? You do know that according to fen history fen tigers are not supposed to be very desirable individuals? Do you really think I'm a fen tiger, Rosie?"

She was prevented from answering this by the appearance of the waiter, and she was vexed that this was so, for she had the feeling that in some way she had annoyed him by referring to him as a fen tiger. By the time the waiter had gone it was more difficult to answer his question, and when a silence fell between them and he did not pick up the conversation again she found it unbearable, and she asked quietly, "Have I upset you by saying that?"

"No, no, you haven't upset me, but the odd thing is, and this may amuse you, I have a strong desire to appear on the good side of your estimation."

She had her fork poised over the lobster cocktail as she exclaimed, "But you do. It wouldn't matter to me what you had done, or what you've been, I feel I know what you are now."

He stared at her across the small table. "You really mean that, Rosie?"

"Yes, yes, I really mean it."

"It wouldn't matter what I'd been or what I'd done, you'd always feel the same about me?"

"Yes."

"Rosie, you're unique. You're unique because I know you really do mean every word you say."

He held her gaze until she became lost to the fact that

154

they were sitting in an hotel in Ely. She only knew that half an hour ago she had become his wife.

But not many hours were to pass before she was to remember her affirmation.

It was nearly three o'clock when they returned home. The sun was shining brightly now, and there was evidence in some fields that the water had gone down slightly. Her arm was held tightly in his as they neared the house, and his laughter now held an excited boyish note as he said, "We haven't met a soul, and here I am bursting to show off my wife." It was the first really nice thing he had said to her, and when, after taking a deep breath, he pulled her to a stop and looked down on her, she could not speak for a moment. Nor could she hold his gaze, for the intensity of his look brought a shyness to her. To cover her confusion, she said, "I want to tell Father and Jennifer. Shall we we go straight over now?"

"No, let us keep that for tonight. Let's bring them over here and have a sort of celebration supper, eh?"

"That will be lovely." She said this to please him, but she would rather have gone and told them straight away.

They went on again, and now he said with brittle jollity, "As soon as I get in, Mrs. Bradshaw, I'm changing and getting down to that dyke."

"Are you, Mr. Bradshaw?" It was a pleasant feeling to know she could exchange playful banter with her fen tiger, so she made bold to add, "So you already prefer the dyke to me?"

"Every time, Mrs. Bradshaw." He had her arm held so tightly against him that she winced and this brought him again to a stop. "I hurt you?"

"A little."

"I'm sorry." His tone had changed and there was a deep solemnity to his words when he said, "I hope I never hurt you, really hurt you, Rosie. I'll try not to, I swear I will."

155

She was all at once overcome with a feeling of sadness and she moved from him, and as they walked the remainder of the way to the house, in silence now, she had the oddest feeling that he would hurt her, hurt her so deeply that she would not be able to bear it. . . .

Maggie congratulated them and blessed them and fussed over them, and she kissed Rosie, and with true Irishism said, "Well, Miss Rosie, ma'am, there's nobody I'd welcome like yourself to say to me, 'Do this' or 'Do that' or 'Hold you hand there, Maggie.' "

When their laughter settled, Michael said, "Where is she?"

"Oh, she's asleep." Maggie sighed. "She's worn out. She started her screaming the minute you left the house. You couldn't have been a stone's thrown away when she started. She was standing in the kitchen doorway there, out of the rain when she first let go, and she pointed this time; she was pointing at something out towards the buildings. But there wasn't a thing to be seen, only the car in the barn. But she yelled her head off as if she was seeing all the devils in hell. It was worse than usual, Master Michael, much worse. I thought I'd go off me head. . . . Aw, there now, I didn't mean to tell you and upset you on this day of all days, but if I were you I'd have her seen to. This is new."

"Yes, yes." He nodded, then, looking at Rosamund, he said, "I'll take her into Cambridge tomorrow. There's a man I've heard of, he specializes in her type. I was going to take her along to him in any case."

"Will you have a cup of tea or are you too full of wine, both of you?"

"I'd love a cup of tea, Maggie." Rosamund smiled at the old woman, then, turning to Michael, drawn by the intensity of his gaze, she asked quietly, "What is it?"

"I was thinking it's a strange wedding day for you."

"It's a wonderful wedding day." Her voice was soft and kind.

"You don't really mind me going off to see about the dyke?"

"No, and I mean it. I love to know that you're going on working, and on the land, on the fens. I've had—as Maggie would say"—she whispered to him now while she jerked her head backwards—"I've had the feeling on me that you'd want to leave here and go off to foreign climes."

"Six weeks ago nothing would have held me, at least I would have said so, and yet now I'm tied myself as if with an iron hawser." Slowly he put his hand on her hair. "A rust-coloured iron hawser."

"It isn't rust, it's copper coloured."

"It's beautiful, whatever colour it is."

She was seeing him now through a thin mist.

"You love it here, don't you, Rosie?"

"I love the fenlands."

He nodded, then in a low voice he said:

> "Your land is my land,
> Its toil and its sweat,
> Its pain to come yet,
> Your land is my land.
> With mud in the meadow,
> Water in the barn,
> Pigs floating down the dyke.
> The Ouse and the Cam,
> Afloat with young lamb,
> You've never seen the like.
> But your land is my land,
> For I've taken your name,
> And the fens are my home,
> Till God stakes His claim.

"That was a rhyme of a fenland bride. It should have come from the bridegroom, shouldn't it?"

She could not answer, her throat was so tight. She

watched him turn away, and as the door closed on him her fingers were pressed to her lips. When she turned, there was Maggie standing with the kettle in her hand, her head on one side, her face abeam as she remarked, "That was nice wasn't it? Oh, that was nice indeed. He can pay a fine compliment, he can that, can Master Michael."

It was half-past six, and Rosamund, dressed in a soft grey, fine wool suit, was waiting in the sitting-room for Michael. She was sitting sideways on the piano stool dreamily touching one key after the other. Michael, changed once more into his town clothes, had just slipped out to have a word with the last of the men, who were finishing early tonight, for it had been a very strenuous day for all of them.

The sitting-room door was open, and she had a view across the hall to the green baize door of the kitchen; and when she saw it flung back and Gerald Gibson come striding through, her tapping of the keys stopped and with a surge of impatience she thought, Oh no! . . . Then, Why has he come tonight? It was odd enough that she should have seen him last night. He usually kept his visits for the weekends. But for him to come tonight of all nights. . . .

She was more nervous than ever now of springing her news on her family and was desirous of getting it over as soon as possible, and here was further delay in the form of Gerald Gibson. But by the time he entered the sitting-room she was on her feet and asking, "Is anything wrong? Aren't you well?"

"I'm all right. Where's Mike?"

"Round the back talking to the men—he'll be here in a minute. . . . There is something wrong. What is it? What's happened?" She went up to him. "There's nothing wrong with my people, not my sister?" She was remembering his enquiries of last night.

"No, it's nothing to do with you; it . . . it concerns Mike."

She was on the point of saying, "What concerns Mike concerns me," but she said almost the equivalent with, "Tell me what it is." Her voice was quiet. "It isn't good, whatever it is, is it?"

"Not for him it isn't." He paused, then, looking at her closely, he said, "You're not falling for him, are you?"

No, she wasn't falling for him; the state of her feelings could only be described in the past tense. She felt annoyed at the question and made no answer, but she continued to look at him as he went on, "I'd be careful if I were you." His voice was very low now. "And I'd get away from here. You don't want to be mixed up in anything.

"Mixed up in anything?" Her voice was cool, and he said quickly, "Oh, I'm not suggesting that you've got involved with him or anything like that, but I'm just putting you on your guard. It's like this. . . ."

"Don't go on . . . please." She felt he was going to say something that would only embarrass them both later. "I think you'd better know right away—Michael would have told you himself when he came in, anyway—we were married this morning."

"My God!" His mouth was wide open and his eyebrows were pushed up towards his hair. He gulped now before going on, "But you can't . . . you shouldn't. . . . He can't marry again . . . she's . . . she's not dead. . . ."

She was staring at him, and she knew that her face was expressing nothing, either of shock or surprise, for she was feeling nothing, only a slight coldness on her neck.

"It's bigamy. He should never have married you. He knew he should never have married you. . . ."

"What did you say?"

They both turned to the french window, where Michael was taking a slow step over the threshold. He repeated in a deceptively quiet tone, "What did you say?"

"I . . . I wanted to see you, Mike. . . . I came straight to see you, but . . . but . . ." He thumbed crudely in Rosamund's direction. "I . . . I have something to tell you."

"What did you say?" Michael was still advancing towards him. His step was slow and each movement indicated a threat, and now Gerald retreated until his back was against the end of the piano and he began to splutter. "A—now . . . look, Mike. Just wait until . . . I tell you. . . ."

Michael stopped when he was about a yard from him and said, still quietly, "I'm waiting."

"She . . ." Gerald wet his lips. "Rosie says you have got married, and . . . and I told her, well . . . you . . . you couldn't."

"You told her we couldn't?"

"Camilla . . . she's not dead. You . . . you said her body was washed up. I tell you she's not dead. . . ."

Rosamund let out a scream as Michael's hands were thrust around Gerald's throat, and she flung herself on him, crying, "Don't! Don't! Listen! Please, Michael! Michael!" As she cried his name for the second time she found herself stumbling backwards across the room, and only stopped herself from falling by clutching the back of a chair.

"You dirty swine!" As Michael's fist contacted Gerald Gibson's jaw Rosamund bent her face in the crook of her arm. The next minute there was a tremendous crash as a table was overturned, and at the same time Maggie's bulk appeared in the doorway and her voice was at yelling point as she cried, "In the name of God, what's come over yous?" Then, with amazing agility for one who was always complaining about her legs, and with strength equally surprising in so old a woman, she flung herself across the room and on to Michael, and her weight alone forced him to release his hold on Gerald Gibson.

"Is it stark staring mad you've gone?" She was pushing at and addressing her master as if he was a young boy

160

again. "What d'you think you're up to? Acting like hooligans." She turned her face now towards the prostrate visitor and demanded, "What bad news have you brought with you to cause this? I knew by your face that it was no good that you were coming with the night."

Gerald Gibson rose slowly to his feet. The blood was running from his lip and nose. He looked to where Michael was standing as if ready to spring again at any moment, and he said bitterly, "I came to tell him that his wife was alive, that's what I came to tell him."

"You're mad, man! She's dead." Maggie turned her small eyes from Gerald to Michael and repeated, "She's dead, you said she was. You buried her, didn't you?"

"Yes, I buried her." Michael's voice was thick and guttural now and still shaking with the rage that was boiling in him.

"You buried her, did you?" Gerald swept the blood from his mouth with his hand. "Well, let me tell you, I saw her not half an hour ago. I was talking to her. Don't forget I knew Camilla. I saw her last night. I've seen her three times in the past week but couldn't believe it. I thought she was . . ." He turned to gaze in the direction of Rosamund. "I thought she was your sister, she's very like her."

"You're a liar! A damned sneaking liar."

"I'm not lying, and you can't bluff me. You knew she wasn't dead. At least you knew the one you buried wasn't her. You hoped it might be, but you had no proof."

"Get out before I kill you."

"Yes, get out." It was Maggie speaking now. "And say no more, not another word." She moved towards him almost threateningly.

When with a dark glare towards Michael he stumbled from the room, Rosamund slid slowly down into the armchair. She had the feeling that she was going to be sick. From under her lowered lids she saw Michael coming towards her and she turned her head away into the corner of the chair.

"Rosie, look at me. Rosie. . . . I said look at me." His voice appeared to be dragging itself up from the very bowels of the fen itself, but she did not obey his command, for, as menacing as his tone was, it could not blot out the voice of a week ago when he had pleaded with her in the kitchen to tell no one of their forthcoming marriage. "I have a feeling on me," he had said, "that dates back to my childhood. Anything I want badly is always taken from me." He had not said, "I've always wanted those things just out of reach, which the law forbids me to have."

"Rosie!" Her head was jolted forward as he gripped her shoulders and pulled her into an upright position. "Why are you believing him and not me? Rosie!" He shook her as if trying to wake her from a dream, a nightmare. "Listen to me. My wife is dead. . . . You don't believe me?" Slowly the grip on her shoulders slackened, and so quietly did he release her that she remained in the same position. He was looking down on her now, his face grey and agonizingly hard. "My wife is dead, I buried her. I carried her up out of the sea myself and I buried her."

"No, no." She shook her head slowly as she listened to her own voice, strange and faraway sounding, saying, "I've seen her. I've seen her looking through that window there." She pointed into the hall, then watched him turn and look at Maggie, and saw Maggie shake her head as she muttered, "In the name of God." She brought his eyes back to her by saying, "Was she like my sister?"

"Yes." His head moved slightly and his words sounded grudging. "There was a resemblance, but she was older."

"Then I've seen her."

"Don't say that." With a sudden movement he was on his knees before her, clutching at her hands. "Whoever you saw, or whatever you saw, it wasn't her. Believe me, Rosie. Believe me. . . ."

162

"Why didn't you want anyone to know we were going to be married?" Her voice was scarcely audible, and her eyes were turned from his.

"Because . . . because . . ." He screwed up his face and bared his teeth as he said, "It was because of what I told you, this feeling, and wasn't I right? But I tell you, you are mistaken about this . . . this other . . ."

"Mr. Gibson . . . he knew her?

"Yes. Gibson knew her, and he wanted her as he wants you." At her sudden recoil he said, "Oh, I've no illusions about my friend Mr. Gerald Gibson. I knew him long before he showed his hand as he did tonight. He's never had any love for me. He would have gone off with Camilla if she would have had him, but he had no money, and she had no use for anyone without money. I tell you, it's some story he's concocted. He guessed about us, and he was out to spoil it."

"No, no, I can't believe that."

"Because you don't want to believe it. You want to back out now." He got to his feet, and she rose too, facing him as she cried, "You know that isn't true."

As they stood with their eyes riveted on each other, Maggie's voice came in between them asking quietly, "How did the child react to her—your wife I mean, Master Michael?'

"React?" He was looking at her across his shoulder. "Why do you ask that? What does it matter?"

"It might matter a lot. For the past week the child has been screaming at nothing, or supposedly so."

"My God!" The words came slow and deep. They had a surprised sound.

As he turned his gaze from Maggie, Rosamund had the impression that he was shrinking before her eyes: she watched him shake himself, literally shake himself, as if throwing off something distasteful, something evil. He walked to the french window and looked out across the fens, and both she and Maggie stood silently gazing at

163

him. When, after a time, he turned he found their eyes waiting for him, and in tones threaded with awe he said, "She's not alive. I know she's not alive, she can't be. But the child used to scream whenever she walked towards her in a certain way, because then she knew she was going to be thrashed. I didn't know it was happening for a long time, this thrashing business. She used to do it when I went out fishing with the men. It was when one of the fishermen's wives saw her at it and she told me . . ." He stood rigidly still, not saying anything for some minutes, and when he did go on he spoke as if to himself. "I set a trap for her—she thought I was away. When I found her at it, I thrashed her with the same stick she was using on the child. It was the day after this that she was missing. Some people thought I had killed her, until three days later they found her clothes behind the rocks half a mile up the coast. It was then young Anthony confessed to the priest, and the priest brought the boy to me, to tell me he had watched her undress and swim out naked towards the point of rock where the waters of the bay met the open sea."

Rosamund could not bear to look at him any longer. Her head was bowed deep on her chest. She was taking into her own body his suffering, his mental suffering over the years.

Maggie interposed, "When her body was washed up, how did you recognize her?"

"I knew her body, Maggie, I knew Camilla's body only too well. I had been ensnared by it. The body that was washed up was hers. If she has followed me here it isn't with her body, but with her spirit. The evil in her that has taken shape. And the fens are the place for spirits."

"Jesus, Mary and Joseph! Will you stop talking like that, Master Michael. I would rather have it that she's alive and on her two feet than imagining her spirit is abroad, and in this place of all places."

164

Rosamund's eyes were tightly closed. He knew her body. The words seemed to cut through her. He came towards her once more, and slowly and gently raised her chin from her breast, and again he said, but quietly now, "My wife is dead, Rosie."

"Let me go home, Michael." The request was whispered, and it was answered by a sudden shout, "No! By God, no! I tell you this is a phantasy. Gibson saw your sister, he imagined it was her. I got a shock myself the first time I saw your sister."

"The child's been screaming, Michael." Her voice was trembling.

"All right, she's been screaming, she's seen something. She's seen the evil that bred her. But my wife is dead."

"Michael . . ." She was appealing to him, holding out her hands. "Michael, do something for me, will you? Will you go down to the boat at the end of the Cut?"

His eyes were narrowed now, telling her nothing, nor did he answer.

"Mr. Gibson thought he saw my sister leaving that boat the other night. Will you . . . will you go and . . . and see who's there?"

"Yes. Yes." He nodded his head slowly. "I'll go to it now, this minute, if that'll put your mind at rest. . . . But you'll wait here until I come back."

She was staring at him, saying neither yes nor no.

He turned from her, went past Maggie and towards the hall door, and there he stopped, and, looking back, he said in a tone which she remembered from the first night she had met him, "I'll expect to find you here when I get back."

She stood by the window and watched him striding down the drive and across the field towards the wood. When he was out of sight she turned to Maggie, where the old woman was sitting on the edge of the chair rocking herself back and forwards.

"I must go home, Maggie," she said.

"No! No! No, Miss Rosie, ma'am, don't do that. Wait as he says. For God's sake, wait."

"Maggie"—Rosamund drew in a shuddering breath—"I believe that is wife is alive. I mustn't stay, Maggie. If I'm here when he gets back he won't let me go. It mustn't happen, Maggie."

"Oh, Holy Mary. That this had to come upon him. He's been dogged all his life. Look, if you desert him in this hour of his need it will be the finish of him, I know it will."

"Maggie, I'm finding it terrible, I'm finding it unbearable. Can't you see I want to stay? With all my heart and soul I want to stay. But I can't, for I know that his wife is in that boat at the bottom of the Cut. Something tells me, something in here." She placed her hand on her breast. "You know yourself that she is alive. The child was not screaming at a spirit, she smelt her mother. Susie may be deprived of normal sense, but she's got a sense that we haven't. People like her can smell fear. She feared her mother and she smelt her. Oh, it's dreadful, it's dreadful." She covered her eyes with her hands, and, almost following Maggie's pattern, she rocked back and forth, before collecting herself again and saying, "I'm going, Maggie; I'm going home. Tell him . . . tell him I'll be back in the morning."

"I'll tell him no such thing. I won't be able to tell him any such thing, for when he gets back and finds you gone the devil himself won't be able to get near him. You don't know the man you've married. He's both God and the devil rolled into one, and that you'll find if you love him. I love him, I've loved him since he was a baby in long clothes. I know him; you've got a lot to learn yet. So start right now. Wait until he gets back."

Rosamund made no answer to this, but, turning from the old woman's bright steely blue eyes, she ran out of the room. . . . She was still running when she reached the swollen river, where, having forgotten to put on her well-

166

ingtons, she splashed through the water to the boat. She seemed to be running still as she pulled frantically on the rope, and when the boat ground against the bank she leaped out and raced into the house like someone flying from the devil himself. She was making straight for the stairs, when both her father's and Jennifer's voices checked her, and she stopped, holding on to the balustrade but not looking towards them.

"What is it, Rosie? What's happened? What's the matter?" Jennifer was by her side, a different-sounding Jennifer, the old Jennifer.

"What is it, my dear?" Henry Morley was at her other side now, his arm about her shoulders. "What's happened? Come on in and sit down."

She flung her head back and tried to shake them off, but her father firmly turned her about and led her into the sitting-room, where, standing on the hearth looking anxiously towards her, was Andrew.

"What is it, Rosie?" He too was bending over her. "What's happened? Has . . . has anyone done anything?"

She could not reply. She could only shake her head and try to stop the lump in her throat from choking her.

"Your feet are wringing wet. Good gracious! Look at you. You must get those shoes off. I'll get your slippers." But Jennifer did not go immediately to get the slippers. Crouching down in front of Rosamund, she added in deeply troubled tones, "What is it, Rosie? What's happened?" Then she asked as if the two of them were alone, "Is it him?"

The word "him" seemed to arouse her father to sudden indignation, for he cried, "If he's done anything I'll go across there and I'll . . ."

Rosamund forced herself to speak. "No. No, please. All of you." She shook her head wearily. "I'll tell you later. Get me a drink . . . tea . . . anything."

"Yes, yes, of course, my dear." Henry Morley almost ran from the room, and Jennifer, saying, "I must get your

167

slippers, you must get these wet things off", rushed after him.

Rosamund was looking up at Andrew.

"In trouble, Rosie?"

"Yes, Andrew. Great trouble."

"Can I do anything?"

"I only wish you could."

"You've only got to ask me, you know that."

"Yes. Yes, I know that, Andrew, and you'd be the first one I'd ask."

"You can't tell me?"

"No. No, not yet."

As she finished speaking her father came hurrying back into the room; he hadn't the drink with him but in his hand he held a telegram form. He was endeavouring to cover his concern with a smile as he said, "This'll cheer you. Andrew brought it over at teatime. It was addressed to you but we opened it, just in case. It's from Clifford—he's coming tomorrow."

He forced the piece of paper into her hand, and her eyes hardly glanced at it. That's all she needed now, to know that Clifford was coming tomorrow. She flung the telegram aside. "He can save himself the trouble." Her voice was angry. "He's weeks too late. Anyway, when he comes I won't be here."

As the two men stood dumbly looking down on her, she asked herself where she would be if she wasn't here. It was silly to talk like that.

Jennifer now came into the room with Rosamund's slippers, and, taking charge of the situation with a quiet assurance that would have surprised Rosamund had she given a thought to it, she said, "Come along into the kitchen; it's warmer there, and you're frozen. You can change in there. Come on now." And she put her hand under Rosamund's arm and helped her to her feet. In the kitchen she pressed her into a chair and actually stripped her wet stockings off, and as Rosamund watched her doing this she thought, Everything's all right with her, anyway.

"It's him, isn't it, who's upset you?" Jennifer wasn't looking at Rosamund as she said this, and when she did not receive an answer she went on, "Don't go across there any more, finish with him. He would have had to look after the child himself, anyway, if you hadn't been here. He's nothing but a great big bullying brute. As I said to Andrew, nothing seems the same since he came back."

No, nothing had been the same since he came back, that was true, and nothing would ever be the same again. She wondered what Jennifer would say if she said to her now, "I married him this morning, and an hour ago discovered that his wife was alive." Jennifer would say, "Well, what do you expect? That's the kind of thing he would do." Yes, that's what Jennifer would say.

It was just on dusk and they were all in the sitting-room. The conversation was desultory, carried on mostly between Henry Morley and Andrew, with Jennifer chipping in now and again. Rosamund had scarcely opened her lips. She longed to be alone, but she knew that if she went upstairs it wouldn't be to sleep, but to sit at the window and think, and brood, and look across the fens towards the house. So she sat with them, not listening to what was said, for all the while her mind was crying out bitterly against what had happened. Consequently, when the thundering rap came on the door it startled the others but brought her immediately to her feet.

Her father, looking at her quickly, also rose. "Stay where you are," he said now. "I'll see to whoever it is."

Henry Morley had left the sitting-room door open, and the three of them stood looking towards it, listening. They heard the latch of the front door being lifted, and then they heard Henry's voice saying, "Yes, Mr. Bradshaw, what can I do for you?"

"*I've come for my wife.*" The voice was not loud, but it

169

was deep and the words came into the room weighed heavily with arrogance.

Rosamund turned from the startled looks of both Jennifer and Andrew, and, putting her hand across her mouth, she went to the window. Her father's blustering voice followed her, crying, "*What!* Now look here, what do you mean? What's all this?"

She heard Jennifer saying, "Oh, Rosie! Rosie!" as if she had heard she had committed a crime. And it was perhaps just that: a crime.

Jennifer was behind her when Andrew said quickly, "Come away, leave her be. Look, come into the kitchen."

"But, Andrew...."

"I tell you, Jennifer, leave her alone."

"I don't believe you." Her father's voice was loud coming from the direction of the hall. Then from the sitting-room doorway he demanded, "Is this true, Rosamund?"

Could she say no? She said nothing, but bowed her head.

When the silence began to stretch her nerves still further, her father said, "Rosie, you should have told us. You shouldn't have done this on the . . . the sly."

"There's a reason why she did it on the sly—I asked her to."

"Well, sir, all I can say to you is . . ."

Rosamund turned quickly on him, crying, "Father, please, please. I'll explain later. Leave me alone, will you, please. Oh, please." She had said me, but she meant us. She watched her father divide his amazed and angry glance between them before turning slowly and leaving the room.

She walked now from the window towards the fireplace. Her body was shaking and she averted her gaze from him. But his next words brought her round to him.

"Have you got her here?"

"You mean . . . you mean Susie?"

"Who else?"

"No. No."

He stared at her for a long moment before speaking again and rapidly now, "I thought she had followed you . . . and you, on this occasion, wouldn't bring her back. . . . And she's not with you?" His eyes were screwed up. "My God! Where can she be then?"

"Rosie!" He was standing close to her, his face not inches from her own and his words were tumbling out. "Come on. I'll have to look for her, but come back with me. We'll talk this over. I'm nearly mad; you realize that, Rosie? I'm nearly mad. One thing on another piling up . . . there's a breaking point. Please. . . ." He had her hands imprisoned and held against his chest.

"What did you find at . . . at the boat?"

"Nothing, not a thing. It was locked up. I waited for over an hour, there was no one to be seen anywhere about. And another thing"—he shook his head slowly—"Camilla loved comfort, she would never have lived on a thing like that. It's a little two-berth cruiser—the whole idea is fantastic."

"I must have time, Michael. It must be proved."

"Proved? I've told you. Do you think that if there was the slightest doubt in my mind I'd do this to you. Look, Rosie." He moved now slightly back from her. "I've been begging and praying, I've been asking and pleading for you to come back. Soon I'll stop doing that and I'll make you. I'll take you whether you like it or not. . . ."

"You can't do that."

"Can't I? You'll see. Well now, once more I'll ask. Are you coming? I've got to go and look for the child. It'll soon be dark. . . . Well?"

She knew as she looked at him he was capable of carrying out his threat. If she said she wouldn't go with him she could see him quite clearly forcing her out of the house, carrying her out of the house, fighting both her father and Andrew in the process. She did not want any more scenes. Quietly she said, "I'll come and help find

171

Susie, then you can force me to stay in the house, that'll be up to you, but I don't consider myself married."

"Don't say that, Rosie."

"I do say it. I'll go on doing so until I have proof that the woman who has been on the fens these last few days is not your wife. And there has been a woman on the fens, I've told you I've seen her."

When he did not answer but stared at her with pain-filled eyes she could not bear to look at him any longer. She could only mutter, "I'll get my coat."

In the hall, near the front door, her father and Andrew were waiting, and, looking towards them, she said, in a voice she tried to keep steady, "The child is missing; he . . . he thought she might be here. I'm going to help find her. . . ." Now she looked directly at her father as she added, "But I'll be back later tonight." She was conscious as she finished speaking that Michael was standing in the doorway behind her, but he said nothing to contradict her statement.

It was Andrew who now spoke. Looking at Michael, he said, "Can I be of help?"

She fully expected a staccato refusal to this offer, but instead she was surprised to hear Michael say quietly, "I would be grateful. It'll soon be dark and impossible to go far with the water everywhere. . . ."

A few minutes later the three of them were going down the steps of the house, and Rosamund, pausing and turning to her father, asked him gently, "Would you look along the river this side?"

"Yes, yes." He nodded somewhat numbly at her, before adding, "But I can't see that she'd be over here—she'd have to cross."

Rosamund did not say, "Anything is possible." Things that were unnatural had this very day been accepted believed, such as an evil spirit walking the fens and causing a child to scream.

172

Jennifer called to her now, "Be careful, Rosie. You'll come back, won't you?"

She made no answer to this, and a few moments later they were in the boat. When they reached the other side it was she herself who said, "It's no use keeping together, I . . . I'll go towards the Goose Pond."

Michael was looking hard at her and he let out a deep breath before he said, "Very well. I'll take the stretch beyond the house towards the main road." Then, turning towards Andrew, he asked him, "Would you mind taking the Cut bank towards the Wissey?"

"Yes, yes, I'll do that. But what if one of us comes across her? Shouldn't we have some sort of signal?"

"I suppose so." Michael nodded briskly. "Whoever finds her can shout, just call out. There's no wind and the voices will carry."

"Very good."

Michael was the first to turn away, and before Rosamund had gone a yard in the direction of the Goose Pond she knew that he was running, and this gave a signal to her own feet. As she ran she didn't question why she had suggested that she would take the road to the Goose Pond. She only knew that from the Goose Pond she could cross a field towards the flood bank and this would bring her out opposite the sluice, and the boat was lying somewhere near there.

As she passed the swollen Goose Pond the geese scolded her and, with necks outstretched, pretended to chase her for some distance.

She didn't run across the field that led to the flood bank but walked somewhat slowly, even cautiously, and as she went she questioned herself as to whether she was looking for the child or the woman. The answer came to her that she was doing both, for from the moment Michael had said that the child was missing her thoughts had sprung to the woman. The mother of the child—the wife of Michael. For, although she felt that Michael believed he was telling the truth when he reiterated that his wife was dead, she herself knew that she wasn't. What she had seen was no spirit of evil; it might be evil, but it was in the flesh, and it was a woman.

When she had climbed to the top of the flood bank she saw that there was no boat away up near the sluice gates. To her surprise, when she looked up-river to the left, she saw that the boat was now at the end of the Cut and looking as if it was actually in the field. It must have been brought up the river recently.

She ran now along the top of the wash-bank until she had almost reached the Cut again, then going down the bank she picked her way through the flooded field until she came within a few yards of the boat. The little craft was pressed against some tall reeds which indicated the bank of the river. It was not held by any rond anchors and was slightly tilted. But its bows, held tight in the reeds, was the reason, she saw, why it was not going adrift. The boat was about twenty feet over all, and the usual type of cabin-cruiser. She was a few feet from its stern when she stopped, becoming almost rigid with an overwhelming sense of fear. In this moment all she desired to do was to turn and speed across the field and over the wash-bank. Her thoughts did not take her further; once beyond the bank she would be safe.

Forcing herself to move towards a window of the cabin, she was in the act of bending down when a voice, coming to her from the bows of the boat, transfixed her. In this moment she was incapable of moving a muscle; even her eyes seemed riveted in their sockets as the voice said, "Don't bother looking through the window, come in; I've been waiting for you."

When, at last, she managed to straighten her back she looked along the length of the small boat to the woman, half leaning over the bows. The woman smiled. It was a quiet smile, and she said, "Do come in."

The voice was beautifully modulated; it had a fascinat-

174

ing sound, only the slight clipping of the words betrayed the foreign accent. As if she were hypnotized, Rosamund found herself lifting one heavy boot after the other over the side of the boat into the small well, and then she was standing before the woman, looking up at her, for she was very tall. She was gazing into a face that looked neither mad nor evil. The woman now said to her quietly, "Go in, go into the cabin."

Slowly Rosamund went into the cabin. It was rather dim inside. It consisted of two single berths, one on each side, which formed seats. At the head of each was a cupboard; between these was a door leading, Rosamund surmised, into a tiny gallery or wash-place, without head-room. It was similar in nearly all its details to the boat Clifford usually hired.

Once in the cabin Rosamund jerked round quickly towards the woman, but she could say nothing. Words were impossible; her feelings at this moment were outraged. This was Michael's wife, and she neither sounded nor looked like anyone deranged; she had even a gentle air.

"Sit down." The woman pointed to the bunk, and slowly Rosamund sat down. "You're small, aren't you? Not a bit like your sister. I've seen your sister."

Rosamund, still speechless, was staring at the woman, and she saw now why she had thought she was like Jennifer—her hair was blonde. But the centre parting betrayed that it had once been brown; auburn, Gerald Gibson had said. But the bone formation of the face was exactly the same as Jennifer's. Yet there the resemblance ended, for the woman's eyes and mouth were different altogether from Jennifer's. What the difference was she did not analyse—she was too disturbed, cut to the heart. Michael had portrayed this woman as a sort of demon, and yet both her voice and manner pointed to her being a gentle creature.

175

The woman now sat down on the edge of the bunk and asked quietly, "So you know why I'm here?"

"No. I only know that you are supposed to be dead." Rosamund's voice cracked in her throat. "Why did you pretend to be drowned?"

"Why did I pretend to be drowned?" The woman looked away from Rosamund now and out of the window, and she gave a little laugh before she said, "You don't know Michael very well or you wouldn't ask that. I would have gone mad, yes mad, if I hadn't got away, and it was no use just walking out. He would have found me and brought me back to look after . . ." She paused and turned her head away. . . . Now she was looking at Rosamund again. "Perhaps you don't know that Michael is, in a sane sort of way, mad. I didn't realize it until he began to have an obsession about . . . Susie."

"Did . . . did you ever beat the child?" She had to ask this question.

"Did I beat the child?" The eyes were wide now, looking into Rosamund's. "Do I look a person who would beat a child?"

Rosamund, looking back into the deep soft brown eyes, thought, No. No, you don't look like a person who would beat a child. A part of her mind was crying loudly now, Oh, Michael! Michael! And it came to her you could both hate and love a person at the same time, hate and love with an intensity that was unbearable.

"Why didn't you come openly to the house and confront him?"

"Confront Michael?" The woman laughed quietly again and it had a sad disillusioned sound. "It's so evident that you don't know Michael. My husband is capable of doing anything, anything he sets his mind to. He brooks no interference, he will sweep everything from his path to get what he wants . . . and at present he wants you. It is as well I realized this almost at once . . . it may have saved my neck."

176

If you don't come I will take you. . . . As his words came into her mind again, she was filled with a shuddering fear. And a deep embarrassment filled her as she looked at the woman whose husband she had married that morning. It was with an effort that she asked, "Then why have you come back?"

"We . . . ll." The word was drawn out, and the woman cast her eyes sideways towards her hands which now lay palm upwards, one on top of the other on her lap. "I might as well be truthful. I can be truthful, there's no reason to be otherwise now. Michael has come into some money, hasn't he? It is evident that I knew about it before he himself did, for as soon as I read about his uncle's yacht being wrecked I knew he would inherit. I haven't any money and I hate not having money." She lifted a rather shy glance towards Rosamund, and Rosamund thought, At least he spoke the truth on this point, anyway. And now the woman went on, "He used to talk to me about the house, and these rivers, until I grew tired. But my enforced listening wasn't wasted, because when I came here I seemed to know them as if I'd been born here. The only thing I was surprised about was that they're not so isolated as he said. I didn't expect anyone to see me, or to notice me, but they did, and that has been the trouble." Again she cast her eyes downwards. "Whoever would have thought that I would have run into Gerald Gibson? You know Gerald, of course?"

"Yes, I know him."

"Yes, I've seen you talking to him. I thought perhaps that you and he . . . Well, well, it wasn't like that at all, was it?" She shook her head and waited for Rosamund to comment, and when she didn't she went on. "I was really glad that Gerald was about. You see, I will be quite frank with you at this point. I really didn't know what I was going to do when I first came here, except about one thing: I had no intention of living with Michael again. Nor, I am sure, would he want me to. I was just inter-

177

ested to know how much money he had come into, and what he intended doing with it. With this knowledge I could gauge how much he would be likely to pay to keep me dead. . . . I knew I would have to prove my identity to him, writing wouldn't do, and yet I was afraid to face him on my own in case he tried to kill me. . . . Oh yes, he'd be quite capable of it; he's threatened to more than once. So then I saw that it was as well I had come across Gerald, for he could be the bearer of the news that I was alive. Also he could witness the meeting between Michael and myself, and be present while we came to some settlement, such as would keep a wife in comfort abroad. It was a better way out than playing dead really." She paused for quite a while, staring at Rosamund, before she added, "That's how it would have worked out if it hadn't been for you. You rather complicated things. . . . Not that I hold that against you. You weren't to know that you were treading on . . . well, a sort of mine. Because Michael is a mine, you know, and he's liable to go off at any minute, for the pin to the detonator is Susan. . . . You . . . you think I'm a bad woman because I . . . I deserted my child?"

"No, no." The words struggled past Rosamund's lips. She didn't think that this woman was a bad woman; weak perhaps, vain perhaps, mercenary, but not bad. But Susan. . . . The name of the child dragged her mind back from the pit of sadness and she muttered, "Susan. . . . Susan is lost. You . . . you haven't seen her."

"Lost!" The woman rose from the opposite bunk. "Since when?"

"This evening. She must have left the house about an hour ago."

"Oh, an hour ago." The woman smiled knowledgeably. "She'll come back. She was always disappearing, but she always came back. One time she disappeared for a full day and Michael went wild. He had the village out look-

178

ing for her, and she walked out of a fishing hut. She had been asleep among the nets."

Rosamund looked up at the woman. Her face had darkened, and her eyes were gazing beyond the boat into the past, and as she watched her Rosamund cried out bitterly inside herself, Michael. Oh, Michael, how could you? Her bitterness brought her to her feet, and she asked, "When are you going to see him?"

"Tomorrow. I'll leave it until tomorrow now. Things will be more straightforward then."

Rosamund couldn't see how they would ever be straightforward again. She said now, "I must go. They . . . they may have found her."

"Yes, most likely." The woman opened the cabin door and, looking with an almost tender look down on Rosamund, said, "I'm sorry this has had to happen to you, because you are nice. There are not many people one can say that to on such short acquaintance. Michael always went for the best." As Rosamund jerked her gaze away, she finished, "Don't worry about the child, she'll turn up. Never fear, she'll turn up . . . somewhere.

"Can you manage?" The voice was quietly solicitous as Rosamund stepped up out of the well and into the half-submerged reeds.

"Yes, yes." She wanted to say something more to the woman but she couldn't.

"Good night."

"Good night."

"Be careful how you go."

Oh, dear God! Rosamund groaned the words to herself as she stumbled through the water towards the wash bank. What must she do? Go and find him and tell him, or let him wait until tomorrow, when the woman—she could not even think the term—his wife, would confront him.

By the time she reached the Goose Pond there was only one point clear in her tortured thinking. If they had found Susan when she got back she would tell him, otherwise she would leave events in the hands of the woman. She showed some knowledge of Michael in this decision, for he was unlikely to make any demands on her, even to insisting that she stay at the house, if Susan was not found. . . .

It was dark when Rosamund came out of the wood and saw the lights shining from the house. Stupidly she had forgotten to bring a torch with her, and so the light was doubly welcome. Doubly because it seemed to bring warmth into her numbed being. Also, for the first time to her knowledge, she was actually afraid of the fenland in the dark.

She was stumbling in her running as she went up the drive, tripping as it were, over her twisted thinking. She wanted Susan to be found. Oh, she did. But that would mean she would have to tell him. . . . If the child was still lost she would be relieved from the hateful task.

As she burst in through the open front door Maggie confronted her from the foot of the stairs and brought out, "You haven't . . .?"

"No." Rosamund shook her head as she stood gasping and holding for support on to the back of a new wing-chair. "Have—have they been back?"

"Yes. Himself and a young farmer who's lending him a hand."

That would be Andrew. Rosamund moved round the chair, still holding on to it for support, and sat down on its edge, and she did not raise her eyes to Maggie when the old woman said, "He's nearly out of his mind. It's too much to happen to a man all at once. God knows I thought he was in for a little peace, and him getting the windfall an' all. But it's touched with the evil finger he is, for nothing's gone right for him since the day he was born. For how other would a man be confronted on his wedding night with the tale that the wife he had buried three years gone was on his doorstep. . . . Did you go

180

down to that boat?" Maggie asked this question under her breath as she moved quietly towards Rosamund.

"Yes." Rosamund kept her head down as she murmured her reply.

"I thought you would. And, like him, you found nothing?"

"Maggie." Rosamund was on her feet gripping the old woman's arm. "I must tell you, I must tell someone or I'll go mad. Come . . . come into the kitchen." She looked around her distractedly before hurrying Maggie towards the green-baize door, and as soon as they were through it she faced the old woman, and in a low breaking voice she began to speak rapidly. "She's there . . . the woman, and . . . and she's his wife, Maggie."

"Jesus, Mary and Joseph. There are evil spirits indeed."

"She's not evil, she's not bad, she's . . . she's nice in a way, charming. . . ."

"She was a fiend."

"No, no, Maggie."

"He said so. Name of God, he told me all about her . . . dreadful things. Things she did to the child. . . . God help her wherever she is this minute . . . he was never a liar, whatever else he was."

"He . . . he is a liar, Maggie." The words were dragged out of her. "She . . . the woman told me why she had pretended to be dead. She was afraid of him. And if she had just left him he would have brought her back to look after Susie. She says he is mad where Susie is concerned."

"Then why has she come back now? Tell me that?"

"For money. She read about his uncle's family being drowned."

"That won't wash. If she's the same woman, why isn't she still afraid of him?"

"She is, but she wants money, she hates being poor. She was very honest, Maggie. You only have to listen to her to know that she is speaking the truth."

Maggie, after staring at Rosamund for a long moment,

181

suddenly raised her hands heavenwards and cried, "Holy Mother, sort this out, will you? Will you sort this out?" Then, bringing her eyes as quickly down to Rosamund again, she demanded, "What of the child? Had she seen the child?"

"No. She seemed amused that I was worrying as Susie had only been missing an hour or so. She seemed sure she would turn up on her own."

"With the water covering everything. Yes, she'll turn up on her own . . . she'll float up. . . ."

"Oh, don't, Maggie, please." Rosamund turned away and, closing her eyes, held her head between her hands, only to turn swiftly again at the sound of footsteps coming from the hall. As she made her way towards the kitchen door, Maggie, thrusting out her hand, checked her, and the old woman's tone was beseeching as she whispered, "Don't give him any more to carry the night, will you."

"I won't, Maggie, if Susie isn't found; but if she is, I must. Listen. There's someone knocking."

Standing in the hall doorway she saw Andrew, and before she could speak he said, "Any news?"

"No, Andrew."

"Has—has he been back?"

"No, I don't think so, not since you came together."

"This is serious, Rosie; unless she has wandered onto the main road . . . well. . . ."

He left the sentence unfinished and they stood looking helplessly at each other.

"What's that?" Andrew had turned to the door again. "There's a light."

Rosamund, standing at his side, looked towards the oncoming bobbing light and before she could make any comment her father's voice hailed them saying, "Hello there."

As she and Andrew hurried to meet him he killed any spur of hope by shouting, "Have you got her?"

182

Neither of them answered until they came up with him, and it was Andrew who said, "No. No sign of her," and then, seeing who was with him, "You shouldn't have come out, Jennifer."

"I . . . I had to. And look, I found this." She held out a mud-covered slipper. "It might not mean anything, it could have been lost some time ago, for it was half buried in the mud."

"Let me see." Rosamund grabbed the slipper from Jennifer's hand, and, holding it close to the lantern, examined it. Her fingers touched the pompon on the front, and separating the wool she disclosed a tiny clean core of blue.

"It's one of a pair she was wearing tonight. They were new last week. Where . . . where did you find it?"

"On the far side of the wood, just off the path leading to our place."

"Near . . . near the water?" Rosamund asked the question quietly.

"No, quite some way off, although it was in a puddle."

"This means she was making her way to the mill . . . to . . . to me." Rosamund looked from the dim outline of her father's face to Andrew, and then to Jennifer, and she ended quietly, "We'd better go in and wait."

Andrew, taking the lantern from Henry Morley, now led the way back to the house, and as they entered the hall again, Andrew, turning to Rosamund, said, "He should know about this." He pointed to the slipper in her hand. "But if I go out and call he'll imagine we've found her, for that was the arrangement."

"We'd better just wait. Come into the kitchen, it's much warmer in there." As Rosamund spoke she startled Jennifer, who was looking around the large hall, surprised no doubt at the elegant pieces of furniture standing out against the undecorated walls.

In the kitchen Rosamund quietly introduced her family to Maggie . . . She thought of Andrew as one of her family. And she realized that she knew much more about Andrew than she did about the man she had married that day—at least, more good things.

There seemed nothing good to remember about Michael Bradshaw except for the fact that he loved his handicapped daughter. And had not this feeling been created in the first place as a form of taking sides against his wife? If his wife had loved the child, then more likely than not he would have hated it.

But all this reasonable deduction was swept aside a few minutes later when, crossing the hall into the sitting-room, a lamp in her hand, there showed up in the perimeter of light the figure of Michael. He was stretched out in a chair just within the french window, and on her involuntary explanation of surprise he turned his head heavily and looked towards her.

"You . . . you startled me. I . . . I didn't know you were back."

He did not rise but said, "I've just got in." And it was the tone of his voice that, for the moment, swept all reasoning and cool thinking aside. There was not a trace of arrogance in it. It was a defeated, dead voice and it drew her to him. His tone did not alter as he added, "I heard voices in the kitchen. I couldn't go in." And then, looking up to where she now stood in front of him still holding the light, he ended flatly, "No one of us had to shout, had we?"

"My sister found a slipper. It . . . it is Susan's."

"Where?" It was as if he had been shot from the chair, and he had to grasp both her and the lamp to steady them.

"The other side of the wood, but . . . not near the river."

"But she must have been going that way. . . . You went as far as the Goose Pond?"

"Yes, as far as the wash bank." She was not looking at him.

184

He released his hold on her and turned from her before he said, "And your friend Andrew?"

"He went towards the Wissey right up to the second cattle barrier."

When he did not speak for some time but stood staring down towards his feet she asked softly, "Can I get you a drink?"

For answer he said, "They can't do any dragging until daylight." He was gazing fixedly at the carpet as if seeing there a map of the action he must take to fill in the time until daylight, and he went on in the same dead tone. "I'll follow the river to the pond—there's thick reed along there—then cut over to the dyke, come out at the bridge, then towards the main road, skirt the back of the house here, and down to the river again." He raised his eyes to her. "Would you ask him if he would phone the police . . . and tell them?"

"Yes." She inclined her head slowly and there was a catch in her voice when she added, "He'll go with you . . . Andrew'll go with you."

"I want no one with me. No one." For a moment there was his old self speaking, arrogance in every syllable. He was facing her squarely now, staring at her, and in only a slightly modulated tone he said, "Do you remember what I said about valuing anything? Once I put any value on a thing it is wrenched from me. 'It'll be all for the best,' they'll say. Can't you hear them? 'Poor thing, it's a happy release,' they'll say. . . . A happy release to lose one's conscience. To lose the only thing that touched the good in you."

She was trembling so much she had to hold the lamp in both hands, and as she turned to put it on the table his voice, although low-toned, seemed to bark at her as he demanded, "Are you just playing the usual female part or are you sorry she's gone?"

"Oh!" She was crying bitterly now. "That's unfair."

"Unfair? How do you make that out? You were, and

still are, ready and willing to saddle me with a wife that I know is dead. As sure as I know that I'm reluctantly breathing at this moment, I know she's dead."

She closed her eyes and joined her hands tightly in front of her.

"Look at me."

She looked at him.

"You went to that boat, didn't you? That's why you jumped at taking the path to the Goose Pond. . . . Well, what did you find?"

She gulped in her throat and twisted her fingers together as she stared through her tears into his grim tortured face. And she knew that if Susan was standing by her side at this minute she could not have said to him, "I met your wife in that boat, and tomorrow she is coming to see you."

The look that he now cast upon her was full of scorn. And the untranslatable sound he made indicated his feelings. When she watched him move quickly towards the french window again, grabbing up the torch from the arm of the chair as he went, she remained as mute as if she had been deprived of speech.

A few minutes later, when she picked up the lamp, she had forgotten entirely what had brought her to the sitting-room. She only knew now that Michael must not be left alone this night. Andrew must go with him. She was calling Andrew's name before she left the room. "Andrew, Andrew. . . . Andrew, Andrew."

It was four o'clock in the morning. The kitchen was stuffy, even hot, and Maggie was asleep in a cramped position in the arm-chair. Sitting opposite to her, Rosamund had succumbed to an overpowering feeling of drowsiness; and although she was sitting upright as if still on the alert for any sound, her head was lolling back against the head of the chair.

Only an hour ago had her father and Jennifer left for

186

the mill. She herself would have gone out then and aided in the search but for Maggie who now expressed real terror at being left alone. "Don't leave me, Miss Rosie, ma'am," she had pleaded, "for I've got the strangest of feelings on me. Like when somebody walks over your grave, you know." So she had pacified the old woman with the promise that she wouldn't leave her until daylight.

Andrew had come hurrying in for a moment around two o'clock when he had asked if there was any whisky in the house. When she had told him yes, he had said, "Let me have some. He'll snap if his nerves are not eased." He also told her they had met the police, who had answered the call almost immediately, but, as they said, there was little that could be done until daylight. And Andrew had ended, "I wish he would believe that and ease up." He had also told her that he had alerted Arnold Partridge from the Beck Farm and he had been with them for the past hour.

It was odd how things turned out, Rosamund thought. Arnold Partridge had been one of the men who had tried to get an order on Michael's land. But for the pressure of this farmer and Mr. Brown from "The Leas", Michael would likely still be in Ireland. And from the bottom of her heart she wished that this was so. For how simple life would have remained if he had never come back to this house.

Rosamund's head lolled to the side now, and her limbs jerked as she began to dream. She was dreaming that she was stepping through the reeds towards the bows of the boat, and when she reached it she turned her back to the little porthole as if to stop someone looking in. It was quite light in the dream, and when a coot began to swim about her feet she felt a surge of pleasure. Coots were rare around here. The bird appeared so friendly that she was stooping to pick it up, when she was pushed forward by a hand coming through the porthole. This brought

187

from her only a mild gasp of surprise, but a sudden startling scream coming from inside the boat made her jump right into the heart of the reeds.

Rosamund was on her feet now. Her eyes blinking dazedly with sleep. "What is it, Maggie?" she cried, grasping the old woman by the shoulders. "Why did you scream? Wake up. Oh, please wake up."

"Oh, God in heaven. Oh, have you got her? She's in there. Oh, Miss Rosie," gasped Maggie, clinging to Rosamund as she strove to draw breath. "It must have been dreaming I was. Oh, but Mother of God, it was real."

It must have indeed been real, Rosamund thought, for the scream still seemed to be reverberating round the kitchen.

"Miss Rosie . . . that boat, I saw that boat, the boat with the woman in it. I could describe it plank for plank. I can see it now, about so big." She pointed to the width of the kitchen. "And two beds it had in it, and then in a cubby-hole of a place at the far end, where I got stuck 'cos I couldn't raise me back, so low it was, there was the child, on a bed affair, not longer than me arm. And I was for picking her up when some fiend-like hands grabbed me round the neck and I was struggling for me life. I screamed an' I screamed and all the while I was aware that the child hadn't moved or spoken. She seemed like dead."

"Now, now, Maggie. Don't distress yourself. Sit back and I'll make you a cup of tea."

"No, no. I want no tea." Maggie edged herself out of the chair and stood gazing towards the curtained window. And as Rosamund looked at her she realized that the dream must have made a very strong impression on the old woman for her to refuse a cup of tea.

"When will it be light?"

"Around about five, I think, Maggie."

"It's no use waiting till then, it might be too late . . . Miss Rosie." Maggie turned and came slowly towards

188

Rosamund. "That wasn't only a dream I had. It was a warning. I've had it twice before in me life. On the night before me mother dropped dead, and her hale and hearty. And almost to the very hour me James was drowned. I dreamed I went down with him into the depths of the ocean an' I screamed; when the boats came back me timing was right. . . . And now I know, as sure I am as there's a God, that the child is in that boat with . . . with its mother. But it won't be there for long—no, it won't be there for long."

"Oh, Maggie, don't. I . . . I was in the boat. There was no place to hide Susie. The bows are so small there is just a little washbasin and lavatory in there."

"She's on that boat, Miss Rosie."

Rosamund saw that Maggie's eyes were not looking at her, but through her, as if she was actually seeing the boat, and her voice matched her eyes with that far-away quality as she went on, "And I saw an omen of death . . . a bird, black with white on its head. It flew away through a little porthole as if it was bearing the child's soul with it."

The coot. The gasp that Rosamund gave brought Maggie's vision back to the present and she said now in her normal voice, "We've got to get himself to that boat. You've got to find him—if not him, then one of the others. For God's sake get into your things and find him."

Rosamund was pulling on her wellingtons even before Maggie finished speaking. The coot and the porthole in the bows of the boat. She was remembering and clutching at the fading points of her own dream. It was strange that both of them should dream about the bows of the boat, the porthole, and the coot. It might just be coincidence; but no, people like Maggie, so near to the earth, had unexplainable experiences. She must find Michael, or someone, and get them to go to the boat.

As she pulled her coat on she said to Maggie, "You won't be afraid to be left?"

"No, not any more. The fear has lifted from me and now I know why. It is no longer round the house, but it is out there, make no mistake about it—it is out there. Go on now, and God be with you. . . . And . . . and tell himself to be careful, will you? And be with him if you can when they meet up."

Rosamund did not answer, for she was already hurrying around the side of the house to the drive.

The darkness now seemed blacker than it had done last night. And the cold was intense enough to suggest winter rather than late July. Rosamund stopped where the broken gate had once leaned and turned her head from right to left. There was no sign of any glimmerings of light. Which way should she go? Towards the mill? That was where they would likely be. Obeying her thinking, she hurried now along the well-known path to the wood, but when she had passed through it and came within sight of the river, there were no flashing torches, or steady beams from Tilley lanterns, indicating the searchers. Nonplussed, she stood for a moment agitatedly questioning. Were they up near the Wissey, or down in the direction of the Goose Pond? If they were near the latter, all to the good, it would be no distance at all to the boat. Would she tell Michael straight away about the woman or tell him of Maggie's strange dream? She didn't know. She wouldn't know what she would say until she met him. One thing she did know. He would not laugh at this tale of Maggie's, for he had a strange faith in Maggie.

When stumbling in her running she reached the Goose Pond it was to find it as deserted as the river bank. Where were they all? What must she do? She couldn't go to that boat alone. But why not? She had been alone before. But that was different. If the child was really in that boat it meant . . . What did it mean? She shuddered and walked on, actually towards the wash bank. She would just look down from the top of the bank and see if there was a light in the boat.

There was no light coming from the reeds to indicate the position of the boat, and the distance was too far away to pick it out with the light from her torch.

She went against every warning feeling in her body when she quietly slid down the wet surface of the wash bank facing the river, and when she was in the water-logged field she directed the torch towards her feet. Sometimes she slipped into a hollow that brought the water almost to the top of her wellingtons, at others she could see the toecaps glittering in the torch light. It was as she stood on one such piece of raised ground that she knew she was near the boat. Slowly she moved the torch to reveal the reeds, and there, just showing above them, was the superstructure of the little cruiser. Even the hairs on her neck indicated her fear as, lifting one heavy foot slowly after the other, she made her way, not towards the well, but to the point of the bows where the porthole was. She was about four feet away when she realized that either the boat had moved its position, or that the water had risen; for she was standing on, or rather sinking into silt, and another step might bring the water into her wellingtons. This could prove serious, as she only too well knew. Caution directed her step to the side, and it was as she slid her foot tentatively into the reeds that the bird rose squawking almost into her face. As she thrust out her hands to ward it off, and at the same time to keep her balance, its fluttering, petrified body was revealed for a second in the light of the torch, and the marking on its head brought a convulsive shiver to her whole body. . . . A coot. Both Maggie and she had dreamed of a coot, and here it was. She had pressed her hand over her mouth to prevent any sound escaping her, and now she waited, the torch switched off, listening for any movement from the boat. . . . There was no movement, no sound, except for the coot, that was still spasmodically expressing its fright from the far side of the river. The woman, if she had been on the river for some time, was likely to be used to

191

night noises and they would no longer startle her, or even disturb her sleep.

Rosamund shivered now with both cold and fear as she stood in the water peering towards the darker blackness of the boat. Now she had got this far she couldn't go back—not now, not after seeing that bird. But she must get her wellingtons off. Slowly she wriggled her foot out of first one, and then the other boot, and she was on the point of stepping forward when the sound came to her. It was a sound she had become used to in the past few weeks. It was the half-moaning, half-whimpering sound that Susie made in her sleep. It stopped, then after a second or two it came again. The child—the child was in there, in the bows of the boat. It was unbelievable, fantastic. . . . Maggie was right. . . . But the woman? The mother? She could not be evil; she could mean no harm to the child. Perhaps she had found her later. Then why hadn't she brought her to the house? Well, how could she? She was just keeping her until daylight. . . . Oh, she didn't know what to think.

"What do you want?"

The voice coming out of the blackness startled her more than the coot or the sound of Susie had done, and she almost fell forward into the water.

"It's me. . . . Rosamund Morley."

"Yes. I know it is. What do you want?"

The question, repeated so flatly, so unemotionally, left Rosamund entirely at a loss. Automatically she picked up her wellingtons, then, pushing through the reeds, made her way towards the voice. She knew that the woman was standing in the well of the boat, and she played the torch over the deck into the well, and not on to the woman's face, before saying quietly, "I've come for Susie."

There was no retort from the woman. It must have been a full minute before she even moved. Then she said as she had done last night, "Come in."

Rosamund found herself hesitating. She wanted to say, "No. I'm not coming in. Hand the child out to me." But then, as if impelled to obey this flat-sounding voice, she waded towards the deck and pulled herself over into the well. And now she did play the torch light on the woman's face, and what she saw turned her shivering into a violent shudder. The face was no longer the one she remembered. The brown eyes held a blank dead look that was in some way akin to the voice. The curving mouth was now a thin tight line, and the cheeks seemed to have sunk in, like those of an old woman.

"Put that out."

After a slight hesitation Rosamund switched off the torch and the woman now opened the cabin door to reveal a night-light burning.

"Don't stand there. Come in."

When Rosamund slowly entered the cabin, the woman clicked the door shut behind her, then in a subtly soft tone she murmured, "Sit down . . . dear, dear Rosie." Both the words and the voice had a really blood-chilling effect. "You know you are very foolish to come back here, don't you?"

It was not in Rosamund's power to make any answer, and after an agonizing pause the woman went on, "It means that I've got to deal with you. You've complicated things for me. When I first saw you I thought, 'She's harmless,' and I decided to leave you alone. . . . That was a very difficult thing for me to do, knowing you were after Michael. But I thought, 'In the end she won't matter, she'll be of no account.' But I misjudged you, didn't I, dear, dear Rosie? That's what he calls you, doesn't he? Dear, dear Rosie. He wants to marry you, doesn't he? Don't get up. You're not going anywhere." The hand that gripped Rosie's arm was like a fine steel band. "I've had to think very quickly in the last few minutes or so. You see, it was Michael I expected to come for Susie, not you. All this talk of waiting until tomorrow was just talk. I expected you to tell him and this would bring him tearing over here. I was to placate him and offer him a drink. . . . Oh yes, I would have placated him. I was going to plead with him. Michael could never withstand a woman pleading with him. It always made him feel extra big, and tough. And once he had taken that drink the rest would have been easy. If he wouldn't drink, I had another way. In any case the result would have been the same—we would, all three, have been found in the boat suffering from an overdose of phenobarbitone, but in the case of Michael and Susie the dose would have proved fatal. It would have come out later that, rather than have me back in his life he had poisoned us. . . . What does the stigma of a bad wife matter when you are the widow of a rich man, and rid of that . . . that freak?" She turned her eyes towards the door leading into the bows. Then, looking back into Rosamund's horrified face, she went on, "She was here all the time. I met her when she was on her way to the mill and you. The sight of me, close to, was quite sufficient to paralyse even her screaming—for long enough, anyway, to enable me to do what was necessary. I used to be quite adept at gagging her in the old days. She helps a lot; she opens her mouth wide."

"Leave go of my arm."

"Sit down then."

"I won't sit down. Leave go."

"There you are, I've let go. Now what are you going to do?"

"I'm going home and I'm taking the child with me." The words sounded simple, even a little silly as she said them. It was as if she were saying to an avalanche, "I'm going to push you out of the way, for the woman before her was an avalanche of terror, of fear . . . yes, of evil. Rosamund was only too fully aware now, and too late, that this was no ordinary woman by whom she was confronted—this was a female Jekyll and Hyde. She had set a trap to catch Michael and she herself had walked into it. Terror mounted as she realized that she was utterly at a loss how to deal with this woman. She had no experience of bad people. She felt gauche, naïve, as she realized that she had little experience of people at all. She had lived almost like a cloistered nun for six years in the mill on the fens. Who was she to cope with a woman of the world, a fiend of the world? For the face before her now had a most fiendish expression. She felt totally inadequate. The only thing she could do was to scream. At the pitch of her lungs she would scream.

There were no portholes in the main cabin, the windows being modern sliding ones, and one of them, Rosamund saw from the slightly fluttering curtain, was slightly open. There was a chance that her voice might carry, for both Michael and Andrew would be on the alert for any unusual sound. She opened her mouth, but her scream was strangled before it even reached her lips. The woman acted as if she had been prepared for just such an emergency. She sprang at Rosamund, and, with a blow that caught her on the shoulder, knocked her flying against the corner of the cupboard that acted as a head to the bunk.

The impact seemed to split her head in two; blackness whirled around her, and she was aware of nothing but searing pain for a moment or two. When the worst of the pain lifted she knew that she was lying flat on the bunk and that there was something running over her face. When dazedly she put up her hand to wipe it away she saw the woman standing tall and straight by her side.

"You're bleeding. But don't worry, that won't bother you for long, and it's saved me a job. Here, drink this." She bent over Rosamund now and offered her a cup.

Slowly Rosamund raised herself on her two hands until her back was supported against the cupboard, and she asked weakly, "What is it?"

"Something that'll do you good. It'll make you feel

good, I promise you. Drink it up." She pushed the cup towards Rosamund's lips.

"I don't want it." With a slow movement of her hand Rosamund warded the proffered cup away. The woman placed the cup on the cupboard, and the next instant Rosamund found herself pinioned against the head of the bunk, with the woman's knee across her legs and her two hands imprisoned within bony fingers. She was pulled upwards into a sitting position, before being flung backwards, bringing her head in contact with the bunk head again. The effect was to knock her almost senseless. The next thing she knew the cup was at her lips, and as she took a gasp of breath some of the liquid went down her throat. It was bitter and vile tasting. She spluttered, trying to cough it up, but when she drew in a breath she again swallowed the bitter, foul-tasting stuff. She did her best not to cough again, but became still when the cup was tilted up to her lips for the third time, and she let the liquid run into her mouth. Then, forcing herself to close her lips and breathe evenly through her nose, she relaxed her body and slumped sideways.

When the woman released her hold Rosamund fell over on to the cushions and slowly she let the liquid trickle from the corner of her mouth. When she was pulled roughly round again there was still some left in her mouth, and she spluttered and coughed, and the woman laughed quietly as she said, "Cough that lot up if you can."

She now brought her face down close to Rosamund's, and, looking into her eyes, she said, "You're going to sleep now. Soon you'll be like her, beyond caring. It won't matter much to you what happens. Are you feeling nice now? It's a quiet feeling inside, isn't it? Nice and quiet inside. I've really been very kind to you, you know."

Rosamund forced herself to close her eyes. Whatever she had taken she could feel no effects of it yet. The woman released her hold and she fell back once more against the head of the bunk, but her head had no sooner touched the wood than she opened her eyes wide, for she was experiencing the most odd sensation. There was a whirling in her stomach, and in her head. There was a weird feeling running down the veins in her legs. The feeling urged her to get to her feet, to get into the open air, but her common sense told her to remain still.

How long she remained still she couldn't tell. It was almost dark in the cabin now. Things were hazy, but she knew that there was a floorboard up, and the woman was on her knees, her hand groping to the bottom of the boat. Then she was standing up again, a torch in her hand, but before it had flashed over the bunk Rosamund had closed her eyes. When she opened them again the cabin was empty. The boat lurched once, and immediately Rosamund knew that the woman had left.

She waited, almost counting the seconds, and as she waited she became aware that she wasn't worrying. As the woman had promised, she was quiet inside. She had a desire now to lie still and not bother; there was a dizzy feeling in her head, her body was numb.

Get up! Get up! Get up! It was Michael's voice, but Michael wasn't here. Get up! Get up! Get up! Somebody was shouting at her. The words were coming only faintly through the thickness in her brain. Get up! Get up! Get up! She was sitting now on the side of the bunk and her feet were covered with water. The boat was sinking. She felt the slightest stir of panic, she had taken out the bung, the woman had taken out the bung. Where was she? Where was the woman? She had gone now, gone to find Michael. Get up! Get up! Get up!

She groped slowly around the door of the bows until she found the handle, then her hands were feeling around in the space before her, but it was her feet that found Susan. Her body, lagging heavy and relaxed against the bulwark, was already half submerged. When she pulled her forward the child fell into the water with a

197

quiet, plonk sound, and then she had her by the back of her dress dragging her towards the main cabin door. She turned the handle and the door opened, but slowly against the pressure of the water. The woman had been so sure of her work that she hadn't bothered to lock the door. The water was over her knees now and round the child's neck. The bows of the boat were almost covered. She tried to lift the child up by the arms, but she couldn't. She felt too dizzy, too dazed. She held on to Susie's collar and supported her against the deck as she peered through the darkening night towards the reeds which were more than three yards away from the boat now.

She never fully remembered how she eased the child over the deck and on to her back in the water. But she did remember the thankful feeling when after only two or three weak strokes her legs and stomach slid against the mud of the bank. She remembered, too, that when she was dragging the child into the reeds she saw that her head was under water, and that she had difficulty in turning her on to her face, and more difficulty still in pulling her along this way, for she couldn't keep her head up, and she had to put her on her back again.

There was a great slow thudding in her head now as if she were going under gas, thud-thud-thud-thud-thud; and with each thud came the words, Quiet inside. Quiet inside. Quiet inside. And she was quiet inside. She just wanted to lie, lie and sleep, but she still went on crawling, tugging the child after her inch by inch. It was the child's sudden spluttering that made her stop. Susie was making sounds as if she was choking. Slowly she pushed her on to her face again and as she did so she thought stupidly, Poor dear, she's sick.

She lay with her head resting on the crook of her arm. She was so sleepy, so sleepy. . . . Get up! Get up! Get up! Michael's voice again. Get up! Get up! Get up! Do you hear? Get up! Get up! Get up! At the last command she pulled her knees up under her and groped towards the child, who was lying on her side. The ground was soggy, but there was no depth of water here.

She must get to Michael . . . Michael . . . Michael. But she was so tired. She stumbled away from the child through the field, but instinctively in the direction of the wash-bank. She was staggering like someone drunk when she reached the top, and as she tried to descend her wavering feet slipped and she slid down the blue clay bank into the field. Again she lay with her head resting on her arm. The thudding was regular now, coming with every beat of her heart. Thud-thud-thud. Get up! Get up! Get up! When she staggered past the pond the geese set up their protest again, and several families of moorhens clucked away in fright from their nests in the reeds.

Michael. Michael. She began to mutter his name. But she must shout it. She must shout. . . . She shouted, "Michael! Michael!" She could hardly hear her own voice, it was so faint and far away. She staggered on, still calling, until quite suddenly she was standing still, and straight. Her head up and her nostrils dilated. She was smelling something. She had never smelt anything like it before. It swept away the quiet feeling inside of her and brought from the dark, dark elemental depths a fear, so tearing, so shattering that she knew that she was no longer herself. It seemed as if her entire being had been shattered, splintered into fragments, all except the core, the elemental core that went back into times dark with forbidden things, times before the soil of the fens ever saw the light of day. In this split second of time she knew why the child had screamed. In this second of time she was the child, and possessed of a sense too keen to be borne. From every pore in her body sound was oozing, screams were shrieking forth, yet there was no sound, no sound at all. Only the presence of the woman, her arms clutching her shoulders, leading her from the path across the fields towards . . . what? She knew where the woman was leading her; she was leading her towards the dyke, towards the end that had been cleared of reeds, because her feet were now dragging and tripping themselves in the cut reeds. The silt in the dyke here would be soft and deep. If you lay still you would sink right down into it. . . . There was no room in her for further terror—she had reached the point where suffering ends.

When the woman pushed her she clutched at the air and fell forward into space and the scream came with her. She could sleep now.

Quiet inside, quiet inside, quiet inside.

10

Quiet inside. Quiet inside. Quiet inside. . . . Oh, she felt sick. So sick.

"Drink this, my dear."

Rosamund shook her head and closed her lips tightly.

"There you are. Open your mouth. That's a good girl."

"I'm sick."

"Yes, you're sick, but you'll soon feel better. Go to sleep now."

Quiet inside. Quiet inside. Quiet inside. . . .

She opened her eyes and saw the woman again and screamed.

"Rosie! Rosie! It's me. Jennifer.

It wasn't the woman. It was Jennifer; Jennifer who had different eyes, and a different mouth, and whose hair was really blonde; it was her sister Jennifer.

Quiet inside. Quiet inside. Quiet inside. . . .

When next she opened her eyes she saw her father, and behind him the sun was shining through the window. He stroked her hair back from her brow and said, "Oh, Rosie, my dear."

Quiet inside. Quiet inside. Quiet inside. . . .

"Come along, try to drink this cup of tea. Come on now, open your eyes. . . . Wider now. That's it."

Quiet inside. Quiet inside. Quiet inside. The voice was fainter now but still there. She looked at the bright face of the nurse bending over her, and this time asked, "Where am I?"

"You're in hospital."

"Hospital?"

"Yes. Don't worry. Come along, drink this. You feel better now?"

"Yes . . . yes." Her voice sounded dreamy and far away. Slowly she put her hand up towards her head, and, feeling the bandages, she said, "My head?"

"That'll be all right. You had a nasty cut. It had to be stitched. There now, is that better?" The nurse put the cup on the locker, then pushed up the pillow under Rosamund's head.

"My . . . my father. He was here?" Rosamund looked round the small room. "And . . . and Jennifer."

"Oh, you remember them being here? But is that all you remember?"

Rosamund tried to think, but it was a painful process trying to think. The voice was still drumming in the back of her head. Quiet inside. Quiet inside. Quiet inside. Why was it saying "Quiet inside" like that all the time . . .? With a sudden movement that sent a stabbing pain streaking through the backs of her eyes, she was sitting upright. "Where is Michael? Michael! . . . Where is he?"

"Now! Now! Don't get excited. You must lie quiet."

"But Michael?"

"He'll be back. He's been here all night and most of the day. He's a perfect nuisance." The nurse's smile softened her words. "He's just gone along to the children's ward. Never fear, he'll be back."

201

"Susan. Where's Susan? Is she . . .?

"Now don't ask so many questions and excite yourself. You must lie quiet."

"But tell me, is she . . .?"

"The little girl is all right. I've told you, she's in the children's ward."

Slowly Rosamund sank down into the bed. The child was safe, Michael was here. . . . Oh, Michael was here. Quiet inside. Quiet inside. Quiet inside. . . . She was sound asleep when Michael next came into the ward.

It was a week later when Rosamund returned to the fens, and to Thornby House. The sun was shining, the water had drained away from the land, and as Michael drew the car up in front of the house door, there was Jennifer and her father, Andrew, and the child, and Maggie, all waiting to greet her. It was too much, too much happiness all at once, and she cried, and everyone was quiet for a while. But at teatime Maggie brought laughter to them all with her humour and quaint sayings, and Rosamund, sitting in thankful peace, was more than grateful to her; oh, more than grateful, and for so many things. If it had not been for Maggie and that something that went beyond the veil of reasoning, they would not all be sitting here now.

In her heart too she was grateful to Jennifer, for now and again Jennifer spoke to Michael, and when this happened Rosamund noticed that he met her sister more than half-way; in fact Rosamund would have said that his manner was charming. She looked at her husband. There was nothing of the fen tiger about him today; he had a gentle, even subdued air about him. Another thing that added to the sum of her happiness was that Michael liked Andrew, and this feeling she knew was reciprocated.

The tea over, she was ordered firmly into the lounge chair facing the front door, and it was from there that she

ater watched Jennifer and Andrew, their figures getting
maller and smaller as they walked arm-in-arm over the
ields towards Willow Wold Farm; and from her seat she
vatched her father take the child by the hand and go in
he direction of the mill. Apparently he had become a
econd O'Moore to Susie. Lastly, she brought her eyes
)ack to Michael where he sat by her side, her hand lost
a his.

"Hullo, Rosie."

"Hullo, Michael." They smiled at each other. This was
he first time they had been alone together except for the
ourney in the car.

"Happy to be home?"

"Yes, Michael, very happy."

"Not afraid any more?"

"No, not any more."

He looked away from her now into the shadowless fen,
and his voice was very quiet as he said, "Before we close
he subject for good and all, Rosie, I want you to believe
hat I spoke the truth when I said that I thought she was
lead."

"I know that, Michael."

Gently he withdrew his hand from hers, and, leaning
forward, rested his elbows on his knees. "I've been over it
a thousand times"—he shook his head slowly—"and I still
can't believe that I made a mistake, although the proof,
God knows, was only too evident. But the body that was
washed up on that shore was as like her body as to be it.
I couldn't go by the face, it was . . ." He shook his head
vigorously. "What's the use? I made a mistake . . . per-
naps I wanted to make a mistake. . . . But who was that
other woman? That's a question that will haunt me from
ime to time all my life."

When he felt her hand on his shoulder he put up his
)wn and gripped it.

"The past is gone, Michael. Don't let's ever refer to it
again."

Even as she said this, Rosamund knew that it would be a long long time before she herself was able to wipe out the memory of the night she was drawn towards the motor cruiser lying at the end of the Cut. And she shuddered now with the thought that, but for a miracle, she would not be here, sitting in the warmth of the evening sun, but suffocated in the silt at the bottom of the dyke.

Why the woman had fallen into the dyke would always remain a mystery. Had Rosamund herself clutched at her in the last desperate moments when she was being flung into space? Or had the bank on which they were standing given way? They had found part of it broken down. Whatever had happened, the woman had been the first to hit the bottom of the dyke, and it was her last terrible scream that had brought Michael and Andrew flying to the spot . . . and only just in time.

It was her father who had given her, very briefly, a summary of the events of that dreadful night. The woman had been dead when they got her out, and she herself almost suffocated by the silt. But she could remember nothing at all from the time she realized that the boat was sinking, and only vaguely did she remember holding the bitter liquid in her mouth and letting it drip into the pillow of the bunk. But she knew now that except for this action she would have lain drugged with the phenobarbitone, as was the child, and been drowned as the boat sank.

"Look at me." Gently she pulled at his ear, and when he turned to face her she made an endeavour to lift his mind from the past events by saying, "Tell me, what did you say to Clifford? Father tells me he came to see you."

He looked at her as a slow smile spread over his face. "Oh, I said a lot to your cousin. I told him he was a fool to have let the grass grow under his feet."

"Don't be silly. You said no such thing."

"Didn't I though? He was a very sad young man when he left here. He's a bit of a fool."

"He's not; he's nice, is Clifford." She could think that now.

"I repeat, he's a bit of a fool—more than a bit, to have ever let you go. Anyway, I made a bargain with him . . . a deal."

"A deal with Clifford? What about?"

"He's selling me the mill."

"No!" She was sitting up now. "Oh, Michael, that's sweet of you."

"Sweet nothing. I've got a business head. We are going to fit that place up into a first-rate factory. Your father and I have it all planned."

"Oh, Michael . . .!"

"Don't you 'Oh Michael!' me in that tone of voice. It's merely a business deal."

"Kiss me, Michael."

Bending forward, he kissed her tenderly on the lips, then said softly, "It will keep him occupied. But he must stay here with you, live near you, because he needs you." He now took her face between his two hands. "Life isn't going to be too easy for you, my Rosie. It's not fair, in a way, because you're starting handicapped. There's not only your father, there's the child, and . . . there's me. And I'll be your biggest problem, Rosie. Oh yes I will." He moved his head slowly. "I'll not let you alone—I know myself—I'll claim your attention like a sick cow . . . or rather bull." He laughed. "And with it all I'll be bumptious, arrogant, loud and demanding. This present quiet demeanour of mine, which is the outcome of shock, won't last. You see, if nothing else I'm my own doctor. Moreover, there's a poison in me that I pour over people I dislike, and the result is that everybody is very uncomfortable, to say the least."

She was smiling tenderly, her head on one side, and her voice had a serious tone as she said, "I know. I agree with everything you say about yourself. And as Maggie would add, 'That's not the half of it.'" She now put up

205

her hands and covered his with them where they cupped her face as she went on, "But you forgot to say that the Fen Tiger is kind and generous. He is also compassionate, and loyal, and very, very loving. . . . Dear, dear Fen Tiger. . . ."

The last words were cut off and smothered against his coat, and his lips, moving in her hair, kept repeating, "Oh, Rosie. Oh, Rosie," and then softly he said, "That morning when I stood outside the solicitor's office and realized I was a rich man I also realized something else, something that hit me with the force of a bullet in the head. It was that all this money, all it stood for . . . comfort, security, travel, even the best attention for the child . . . meant nothing . . . less than the muck under my feet without you, you and your love for me. And I became terrified from that moment of losing you."

"Well, you didn't, darling."

"You'll always try to keep on loving me, Rosie, even at my worst?"

"I'll love you best at your worst."

"Oh, Rosie. Things will never be easy for you, you're made that way."

In the darkness behind her closed lids she saw a picture of the coming years. As he had said, things would never be easy for her. Money in her case would not make all that difference, for money could not lessen the demands he had mentioned. The demands of her father, of the child, and . . . of himself—her Michael. They all wanted loving, mothering, but Mike most of all. Would she, if she could, change the picture that she saw threading the years? No, not one little iota of it. She had been made to give. That's what brought her the most happiness—giving. She had been made for others to lean on, but the burdens she had now to bear would be light. Life would be light, for she had an overwhelming compensation—she had the unstinted, passionate, demanding love of this man . . . her Fen Tiger.

THE END

CATHERINE MARCHANT IS BETTER KNOWN AS CATHERINE COOKSON

THE LONG CORRIDOR by Catherine Cookson

To outsiders the life of Dr. Paul Higgins appeared to be a contented one. He seemed to have everything a man could want. But the façade that Paul and Bett Higgins presented to the world concealed a welter of hate that grew worse with the passing years.

Between Paul and Bett stood the barrier of the past of secrets that, were they known, could affect everyone about them.

0 552 08493 X—40p

FEATHERS IN THE FIRE by Catherine Cookson

Every once in a while circumstance traps a group of people in a pattern of tragedy and violence from which they struggle vainly to fight free. Thus it was with the Master of Cock Shield Farm, Angus McBain, who was too easily tempted to sin, too sinful to escape a hideous retribution . . . and Jane his gentle daughter · who devoted her life to caring for her deformed young brother . . . Amos, the legless child whose tortured spirit transformed him into a demon capable of every cruelty—even murder . . . and Molly Geary, the 'fallen' servant girl, whose love for the child she had borne in shame gave her strength to become a truly courageous woman . . .

0 552 09318 1—65p

A SELECTED LIST OF FINE NOVELS
THAT APPEAR IN CORGI